THE SERPENT AND THE SWAN

Also by Ashland Pym

<u>Non-Fiction</u>
The <Virtual> Myth Conservancy

Find more at

www.pymspen.com

THE SERPENT AND THE SWAN

Ashland Pym

Night Sea Press

GALWAY, IRELAND

For my Grandmother,
Carol Pym

CONTENTS

CHAPTER ONE

✳ UNNATURAL

The king no longer enjoyed his rule now that the queen locked her doors against him and the crops rotted in their fields. Now people expected things of him, and all he cared to do was hunt.

But, as the farms and the towns nearest the castle withered, so too did the King's Wood. Some beetle that bored into the bark, the groundskeepers told him. They wiped out trees in the hundreds. Wolf and bear, boar and deer, all died out or fled. All that remained for the pleasure of the chase were the small prey that still scratched a living from the dirt and dead leaves.

The kingdom had once been one of abundance. To claim his right to rule, King Torvald had defeated one of the Otherworld Kings, and since that day the fields had overflowed at every harvest. It was the perfect rule for a monarch of leisure, as he was. Game was never hard to find in the King's Wood. No strife distracted him when he desired to abandon affairs of state for the pleasure of the woods. He spent more nights in a tent than in his own chambers. And when he returned with his kill there would be a feast to follow, and pleasurable company to finish. It was all part of the Hunt.

Leisure came to an end when his advisers insisted that he protect the country's future and produce a legitimate heir. The hunt for a queen was blessedly short; a neighboring ally sent Gyda to him at his first courting summons. Princesses from every country arrayed themselves for his viewing pleasure that he might secure their fathers' fortunes with a wedding vow, but she was the prize doe among them and he would stop at nothing to catch her.

Catch her though he might, tame her he could not. She was an eager wife at first, but she had little interest in the hunt and soon she preferred to stay at the castle and read her books. He commanded her to attend but she refused, and so he had her books removed. When he discovered her cousins had brought her more, he had them burned. Her preference for her own company over his galled him. That night, the air still heavy with smoke, he went to her for his marital rights and she barred him from her chambers.

To compound the king's frustrations, the first signs of blight appeared soon after. The castle orchards failed to fruit. The kitchen gardens sickened and withered. Within months, no game could be found in the King's Wood and the trees were dying. Lords from nearby towns reported that their fields were festering and the livestock had gone barren.

The growing threat of shortages and loss of economy drove King Torvald more frequently to pleasurable distractions. However, the lack of large game upon which to vent his spleen only forced him further into the Wood, where nothing but anger grew. He could command crops to grow, but they would not listen. He could wear his crown to visit blighted fields but could not control the pestilence. If it continued into next year, his once-rich kingdom would be reduced to merely sustaining itself, with no exports. And with no exports there would be no money to buy pretty trinkets to regain favor with his once-amenable queen.

She was another that would not be commanded or controlled. In the year since their marriage he had bought her hundreds of the finest gowns, but she continued to wear the drab garb of her homeland. He ensured her ladies-in-waiting were pure, trustworthy women who safeguarded her wellbeing for him. He kept unworthy people from stealing her attention. And yet she continued to withdraw from him.

Of late, she spent more and more time with her cousins. They had come with her from their native country as part of her bridal entourage and now they lived in his castle, ate his food, drank his wine, and poisoned his wife against him—he was sure of it. She would not wear the dresses he gave her, so he had her old ones burned, only to have them lend her their own. He sowed petty jealousies between them, but they would not turn on one another. She spent few meals in his company and fewer nights in his bed, preferring *their* company to pray and reminisce of their homeland. He should strike their heads from their shoulders for it. But he was too kind a man for such extreme measures—a kindness Gyda refused to return.

He had no memory of such violent fantasies entering his thoughts before she came into his life. She filled him with vitriol. The closer he tried to keep her, the further she retreated from him, and what love she may have harbored before had clearly turned to disdain. Her cruelties toward him were turning him cruel in kind. The resentment he felt for how she had changed him hovered ever in his thoughts.

And so a suspicion surfaced that the blight that ruined crops and sickened livestock had been brought by the cousins. Inventing the rumor had been a drastic step, but what option was left to the king? It made no matter to people that the native country of the queen and her cousins suffered no such curse, and so they could not have brought it with them. Prejudice and fear had done its work, and the cousins were forced to quit the kingdom. King Torvald needn't lift a finger to see them gone; popular demand did his work for him.

He would have his queen to himself again, a beautiful doll for him to dress and command and display as he saw fit.

Yet Queen Gyda showed an intelligence and cunning befitting a man, he thought. It did not take her long to realize that he was the source of the rumors that had exiled her family; she accused him of perfidy and threatened to permanently deny his marital rights to ensure she never produced him an heir. He had no defense but to feign ignorance and hurt and beat a hasty retreat for the hunt.

But today even the hunt did not soothe King Torvald.

Voles made for excellent target practice, but they did nothing to quell his anger. Anger that she should be so ungrateful that he desired her company. Anger that she should catch him out, and so quickly. Each twitch of dead leaves might be new prey, and each time he imagined the head of one of those wretched cousins as he loosed another arrow. But these voles, stoats, and rabbits would not satisfy. He needed the smell of sweat and blood and fear that came from chasing big game, and he would have it. Exhausted as his hunting party was, he pushed them still deeper into the King's Wood.

A flash of white among the barren trunks ahead of him drove his queen from his thoughts. He slowed his mount and squinted. Yes, something large picked its way over roots and rocks with a sure-footed elegance even his horse couldn't match. It stopped at a stream and lowered its head, giving him a clear view of the hind. A good predator knew he should not hunt a female in times of scarcity, yet he readied his bow anyway. It had such an otherworldly beauty, and he had no power to stop himself. It would be his.

The deer lifted its head and turned to look directly at him. He could see steam rising off the sweat on its flanks and in the gust of its breath. The light that filtered through the sparse canopy overhead reflected from its milk-white body, giving it a halo against the brown and gray of the forest. Frightened green eyes fixed on him.

Such tangible fear tempted him. It could have fled, but instead it all but beckoned him to take aim and put an end to its miserable life. To drag its body across his saddle and parade it home. To mount it as a trophy in his throne room as proof of his conquest, as his wife had once been. But he would ensure that this trophy, unlike the queen, would remain mounted.

As the king took aim, the hind bolted. He spurred his horse after it, leaving his retinue behind. He kept his eyes on the white flanks ahead of him as his quarry bounded over rotted logs and darted through the increasingly narrow gaps between the trees. The Wood was not this expansive; he should be through the far edge by now. This area should not be here. Death had not reached this strange part of the Wood and he welcomed the rich greens of ancient forest. Here, early summer was alive in the buzz of insects and birdsong. Ivy covered the ground in a thick carpet. The broad leaves of sycamore trees, taller even than the gnarled oaks, crowded the canopy and blotted out the sun. Small creatures scattered as the hind crashed through the ferns, the king's horse thundering after it.

The path dwindled to less than an animal track, and he was jolted with every step caught on rock or root. By the time King Torvald halted, his mount's flanks were wet and its mouth frothed. It was too dark to see clearly and branches hung so low they threatened to pull him from his saddle. What little light pierced the forest canopy was obscured in building mist. Nimble as his horse was, it would soon break a leg or lose its rider. He could go no further, but on foot.

King Torvald feared that he'd lost his prize, but soon heard movement ahead of him. Without the noise of his horse, he might sneak up and take it unawares. Working in silence, he nocked his arrow and crept through the bracken. In the narrow gap of the trees was a flash of bright white in the dull gray mist. With slow, steady breaths, he took aim and loosed.

The scream that cut through the forest was that of no hind, but a woman.

The king ran, dodging roots and grappling branches, until he burst into a clearing. A Lady All in White lay crumpled against an ancient spiral-carved stone, a crimson bloom spreading from the arrow deep into her thigh. Raven hair obscured a face the color of shadows as she sobbed, her hand leaving a bloody print on the stone.

King Torvald hesitated. His quarry was nowhere to be seen, and he did not trust the place he had found himself in. It was not his kingdom, that was certain. Caught between stream and stone, he felt on the edge of one world but not quite into the next. Nor did he trust that the woman in front of him was human. His hand fluttered to his sword hilt—he had come for prey, and what more dangerous prey than the Fair Folk? The fae were famously vicious, all the stories said. The women most of all, for all their cunning. Demure one moment and devouring the next. His muscles coiled to visit upon this fae woman the rage he secretly wished to visit upon his cunning and ungrateful queen.

The Lady All in White looked up and he met wide, emerald eyes.

In the dark recesses of his spirit, something quelled and fell silent. She was small and dark, her beauty opposite in every way to Gyda's. Had she looked so a few moments ago? He couldn't remember and didn't care anymore. He felt as if a hand had passed over his eyes, and in a rush his rage died.

He removed his sword belt and laid it carefully at the clearing's edge, followed by his quiver, his bow which he unstrung, and his knives for skinning and gutting. All on display in a neat row. She did not react as he crossed the grass, but flinched as he crouched beside her. Compassion bloomed in his breast—a sensation he'd not felt in over a year.

"Forgive me, My Lady," he said, "but I am the cause of your suffering. I would undo this harm and place myself at your feet in penance."

The Lady All in White said no word, but looked up from her tear-stained hands and nodded. As gently as he could, King Torvald gripped the arrow's shaft and pulled it from her thigh, using a clump of moss to stem the fresh flow of blood. She made not a sound, and for a moment he feared she might be an animal in disguise, but she soon spoke in the voice of a human woman.

"You freely give aid where you might have a trophy instead. In gratitude for your not having violated this body and this ground, I will pay you the same respect. I ask only that you stay with me until I am able to walk again and return home."

Her face was kindly, with a smile that hovered about her lips. That smile warmed him; his queen never smiled at him anymore.

The eager king acquiesced and spent three days and nights at the fairy woman's side.

Never had he felt such comfort and joy, not even in his youth. Come the third night, however, his happiness turned cold. As he gazed down on her sleeping face, he feared that his fairy woman would soon desert him for her own world. At her side he felt a peace he'd not known since he was but a prince. Her arms held far more pleasure for him than the queen's bed. He feared that losing her would be to lose this bliss and leave nothing but sorrow and longing to fill his remaining days. He could not let that happen. Come morning, if he could not convince her to return with him, he would find a way to make her.

On the dawn of the fourth morning, however, he woke to find the mist lifted and the Lady All in White gone. His horse was grazing by the clearing edge; it must have wandered the last three days to find him. The trees were younger and thinner than the black forest he had pushed through to find this place, and a clear path opened up not far away. Collecting his weapons and mount, King Torvald followed the track to wherever it might lead. Soon the surrounding trees gave way to decay, leaning against one another or littering the forest floor. When he broke through to daylight, he discovered that he was at the foot of his own castle.

The king went first to his queen to confess his indiscretion and beg forgiveness, though in truth he only desired to spark a modicum of jealousy. It would mean she still cared. Instead, he found that she had hardly noticed his absence, only that he'd not pestered her in days. Angry and lonely, he attempted to return to the clearing where he had met the Lady All in White.

Though he searched the Wood for a month, he never again found the path to lead him there.

Thus, King Torvald sent out his knights to search for every ancient grove and every whisper of the Fair Folk—to find the Lady All in White and bring her to the castle. Queen Gyda, either seizing an opportunity to gall her husband, or perhaps seeking to spare the Lady All in White the fate of the queen's same prison, sent her knights meanwhile to destroy every ancient grove they found and punish those who kept the Old Ways. Anyone rumored to have dealings with the Fair Folk, noble and peasant alike, was imprisoned or sentenced to death in accordance with their station. Any who pleaded their case to the king in hopes of clemency were questioned about the Lady All in White and, when they could give him no information, were left to their fate.

Nine months after King Torvald's journey into the Otherworld, at the stroke of midnight of the first day of the second month, arrived at the castle a Knight All in Red and a Knight All in Black. They were unarmed; but between them carried a basket and spoke no words but to demand an audience with the king. After much fuss from the steward, they arrived before the patriarch.

"We come from our Lady," they said in chorus. They laid the basket at his feet and bowed from the room. No one saw them leave the castle grounds, but soon afterwards they and their horses were gone.

King Torvald looked into the basket and found there an infant with a head of black hair and emerald eyes. As he loosened the swaddling cloth to see whether his heir was a son, he recoiled. In place of the babe's left arm was a snow-white swan's wing.

The king sat back heavily and stared at his deformed daughter. Any hope for an heir died, for he knew his people would never accept this inhuman creature as their future queen. Her very existence reflected upon him, and he felt his throne tremble.

"Unnatural," Queen Gyda sneered when she saw the child. "God is punishing you for your infidelity."

King Torvald shifted his gaze to his wife. Where she stood he saw a cold, heartless woman in place of the mother of his only child. He gathered the infant in his arms. "I will call her Cygna," he said. "My own little Swan Maiden."

"You cannot think to let it live. No doubt its mother sent it here because its own people would tear it limb from limb. Why should we be forced to rear it?"

"And what you have me do with her?"

"Drown it. Feed it to the dogs. Anything would be kinder than letting it live."

"*She* is mine. I will see no harm come to her. Try, and I will have your head struck from your neck."

The queen lifted her chin. "*She* has no place here. What sort of life will she lead? Everyone will fear and shun her. Look at her—she is already torn between two worlds. She will never fly, and she will never belong. She is nothing more than a broken princess who will resent that she cannot be human. Put her out of her misery now."

"I have no other heir. We are as barren as the fields outside this castle."

Gyda stiffened, but forced herself to soften her features and offer a smile. She reached out a tender hand to his.

"Come to me tonight. God has punished you, but He is giving you a chance for a true heir."

Interested as King Torvald was in his wife's sudden willingness, he refused to put an end to his half-human progeny. She was given to a wet nurse and put under guard. Gyda came to her husband with renewed interest and nine months later, at daybreak, the Princess Aila was born. Her duty done, the queen once more retreated in icy disdain, and the king marveled in his two daughters, one like dusk and the other like dawn. Aila of the rosy-blonde hair and blue eyes, Cygna with raven hair and eyes of green.

CHAPTER TWO

BETWEEN WORLDS

To Queen Gyda's dismay, a natural daughter did nothing to deter King Torvald's interest in his firstborn. If anything, he showed his little Swan Maiden favoritism. She was a new doll for him to dress and mold as he saw fit.

Try as he might to keep his daughter's existence a secret, his frequent disappearances could not go unnoticed, and rumors spread with distressing accuracy. He assumed that her wet nurse, Betild, was the source, so he locked her away with the baby and sent a royal guard to inform her grieving family that she had been eaten by a wild animal while walking the King's Wood.

It was Betild's own mother who answered the door, and she listened without a word as the man described the manner of her daughter's death. He gave a bloodied shift as proof. Betild's mother ran her hands over the stiff brown stains as the guard repeated the king's personal condolences. She remembered every stitch of the forget-me-nots she'd embroidered to strengthen the seams. When the guardsman was gone, she washed what blood she could out of the linen and used it to swaddle her now motherless granddaughter.

To the outsider, however, Princess Aila was the king's only child and heir. Queen Gyda hoped to keep Aila in ignorance, but as the child grew into the age of curiosity she was fascinated by the servants' gossip of an unnatural older sister locked away somewhere in the castle. It also did not escape her notice that her father was rarely to be seen. She took every opportunity to slip away from her nursemaids and search from dungeon to towers for any mysteriously locked doors or unexplained guards.

To quell her daughter's interest, Gyda filled Aila's head with stories of the cruelties of the fairy race and all the horrible things that would be done to her if she met one. Even a half-breed. Even a sister. Queen Gyda commissioned storytellers to revive the old fairy tales and compose ballads and plays illustrating the treacherous nature of the fae and their delight in human prey, popularizing a new genre of entertainment both in Court and around the hearth. And as the pestilence that rotted the fields spread further through the kingdom year after year with starvation hard on its heels, people found an explanation for their misfortunes.

It either was lost to memory or it did not matter that King Torvald's seduction by a fairy woman and the arrival of their progeny had come more than a year after the first signs of blight. Mobs aided the queen's knights as they dragged suspected worshipers to the pyre. Betild's family, who still suffered from the loss of her income, had no explanation for how such a hard-working girl would have had time to wander the King's Wood. They listened to the fireside fairy stories, and to the rumors of the Swan Maiden, and knew it was no wild beast that had devoured their beloved Betild. It could only be the king's fairy get. And soon their friends and neighbors knew it, too.

King Torvald responded to this fearmongering by eliminating any who had ever seen Cygna's true form and denying her existence. Her only companion was her governess, imprisoned with her, and only he, her doting father, might come and go from her rooms. She did not remember Betild enough to ask what had become of her once Cygna was too old for a wet nurse.

The king protected Cygna by isolating her, but it pleased him that in so doing he had no other rivals for her affections. She could not help but learn of her stepmother and half-sister through her lessons in history and government, but he assured her of their cruelty and hatred toward her to keep her from longing for them. He made no mention of her true mother or her heritage, but she could not help but make a connection between herself and the Lady All in White her father spoke of seeking, and of the terrible stories of the fae her governess told at night.

It could not escape Cygna's notice that she was different to her father. She was forever in trouble with her governess for tearing one arm off her doll and attempting to sew a wing in its place. When pressed, her teacher would tell her only that her wing was a curse for her father's sins and she needed to cleanse herself of its stains.

For her, it was a different curse. With only one wing, she could not fly from her window to explore the lands she looked out on, or find the lands she came from. And with only one arm, she could not walk among the people as one of them. Nor could she quite decide which she wanted more. But she knew it did her no good to wish or dream for the future. For what future could she possibly have, unable to appear in Court and locked away from prying eyes? And what good would it be to fly away when there was no safe place to go?

As she entered her teens, the arrangement of being locked away was no longer practical. After much arguing and coercion, King Torvald agreed to let his daughter out of her rooms if she met his demands. Cygna would not be permitted to roam freely; on those rare occasions she was allowed into the castle proper she would be escorted at all times by her governess, who was eager to be free of her prison, and the only two guards the king trusted enough to the task.

To have gowns specially designed to accommodate her wing would be to acknowledge Cygna's Otherworldly heritage. Instead, the king ordered her to tuck her wing under her bodice so that the sight of her deformity would offend no one. She would never be formally introduced, though he had no delusions; he knew that the people could not help but notice a closely guarded girl with one arm who haunted the fringes of court. Still, the queen would deny Cygna's association and her place. The princess was strictly forbidden to speak to her.

The first time Cygna emerged from her rooms was to stand at the edge of a banquet. For Cygna and her father it was her thirteenth birthday; for Queen Gyda and the Court it was a Tuesday. Compared to the relative silence of Cygna's rooms, the musicians and the chatter and the clinking of glasses and the sounds of eating as they echoed off the marble columns were a cacophony beyond any nightmare. She had come curious to find anyone who resembled her—anyone who had any deformity beyond the perfectly beautiful forms of her father and her governess and the illustrations in her books.

In this press of bodies and colors and feathers she saw no two forms alike, but they wore masks and costumes and the trappings of what they found so horrifying but was a part of her own body. No human faces turned to her, but disguises of exaggerated and animal proportions. More false faces hid behind feathers and flashing jewels, looking every which way and never settling their attention anywhere for long.

Music bolder than the tinny mockery from the box on her bedside table swallowed all the rhythmless noise of the people and consumed it until threads of conversation and forks on porcelain, too, found their tempo. They found their beat in Cygna's blood, but she didn't know the steps, and the rhythm of the dancers as they wound knot-work art in an invisible labyrinth around one another was too perfect a movement to interrupt. She'd have fled the overwhelming stimulus for the silence and solitude she knew, had it been not for her first taste of music and the beautiful unison of so many bodies moving with its tempo.

And yet Cygna could see entwined around each mask, in an embrace both protective and predatory, a ghostly partner, a shadow, a distorted echo in colors both duller and more vivid. She sensed rather than heard echoes that sounded of blood-lust battle cries dying off one by one until there was nothing left but sobs, then silence. Perfumes that should have smelled of roses carried the scent of cold damp earth from inside a crypt. She glanced up at her father at his banquet table but the king, too, had a shadow-self wound around him. Like the others, it was more of an impression than an actual presence, but though she saw no face she felt it stare possessively around the room, hunting.

Overseeing the writhing cacophony of the bacchanal, a statue towered behind the king's throne. It needed no beastly shadow-self for it already was bestial, like Cygna. Its face was the elongated, skeletal maw of a horse held upright by a long, sinuous neck. Its body was human enough, though, one hand holding aloft a branch and the other broken off. Her father had boasted to her at every chance how he had earned his throne by challenging an Otherworld King to a contest of strength and wits. King Torvald had prevailed in the end when he had tricked his rival into falling under an enchantment that turned him to stone. Though it was the only still figure on the room, it drew her attention again and again. There was no ghastly specter that hung around it, but she had the sense that it, more than any other curious reveler, had its focus on her.

Cygna fled after only a short while attending her first ball, unable to withstand the noise and the press of the bodies, the painful way her wing was twisted under her dress, the heat and the costumed mockeries of her bestial form, the unnatural visions and the stare of the dead king.

It would not, however, be the only ball she was forced to endure. Though the visions did not return with such oppressive force, she occasionally saw a shadowed dancer from the corner of her eye or caught a cryptic scent as someone passed her. She found little contentment in donning a mask for these banquets; she disliked that she could see no one's face nor recognize a single costume from night to night. She spent all her time outside her little sanctuary with people she would never know.

It was easy enough to steal a copy the governess' key. The castle blacksmith took a bribe of one of her rings for work and silence. When she could, Cygna evaded her governess and her guards to wander alone, first within the castle halls and then into the grounds. She wanted to catch a glimpse of her father in his own world, of the stepmother and half-sister she never met face-to-face. Whenever she glimpsed Aila, however, she was being ushered along by her own guards, hurried from place to place much the same way Cygna was. Queen Gyda, however, trailed her guards and the ladies-in-waiting behind her as though they were under sufferance. The first time Cygna tried to introduce herself, she earned only a sneer and an irritated wave of a hand as the queen brushed past.

After that, however, Queen Gyda made an unexpected appearance in Cygna's rooms. She dismissed the governess, who had been in the middle of yet another dry lecture on import and export, and sat in the chair nearest the fire. Cygna sat at her writing desk, eager but also too afraid to speak.

"I did not say you could be seated," Gyda said, and Cygna got promptly to her feet. "So, here you are. The last time I laid eyes on you from this close was the day you arrived here. I had hoped not to do so again. Turn around; let me see you." The Swan Maiden pivoted slowly in place. "I'm glad to see they've done something to hide that wing of yours. You're coming into womanhood very well, I suppose. Your face is a bit too sharp, but I hope you will grow out of that; I suppose there's nothing we can do to make your complexion fairer. You might even be passing pretty one day, were you not so deformed. Not as pretty as my Aila, understand. You're not to impose yourself on her. Do you hear me?"

"Yes, Your Majesty," Cygna managed through a throat constricted with terror and disappointment.

"I suppose now that you're allowed out you expect to be a part of the family. This will not be the case. You have nothing to do with me, or with Aila."

"I know that, Your Majesty."

"Do not interrupt. As your father has seen fit to give you notions of freedom, it is only natural that you would give in to curiosity. Be sure it does not lead you to draw unnecessary attention to yourself or your association with us." She stood and smoothed her gown. "I do not know what future your father has in mind for you, but it can have nothing to do with us. I do not say this to hurt you. You cannot risk anyone finding out what you are. It would be a danger to us, to this country, and not least of all to yourself. It would have been kinder to send you back where you came from, wherever that is, but your father wanted to keep you. And I do not doubt you've suffered for it. I am genuinely sorry for it. I am no stranger to being locked away, made to wear painful gowns for the pleasure of others, not knowing what thread fate spins." She paused, and Cygna could see that she was calculating her words. "I am sure you long for a mother figure. Do not expect to find it in me. But as there is no one else, I suppose you may, on occasion, speak to me. Do not seek me out in public again. If you must call on me, and I hope that will be rare, send word. I will come to you when I have a spare moment."

She left, and Cygna felt lonelier for it than she had before she'd known that a mother was something she was missing. The queen's cold pity angered and unsettled her, and before her governess could come back, she slipped out of her rooms to escape the confinement of those walls and Gyda's words.

It was during a delivery of foodstuffs and stores from one of her father's allies that she was able to steal some boy's clothing from a consignment of woolen goods. A well-to-do merchant had set his thick cloak aside as he haggled with the castle steward and Cygna took that, too. In such drab clothing, and with the cloak to hide her empty left sleeve and the odd shape her bound wing gave her torso, she could move freely within the city. Without her Court mask, no one recognized her.

At first a few of the young men paid her too much attention. A clean-faced girl with shining black hair and emerald eyes was unusual enough, but the darkness of her complexion, the sharpness in the angles of her face, the dark red of her lips, and the cutting looks she gave those who came too close compelled them to hound her whenever she walked the streets. They fell in behind when they spotted her, shouting out to ask for a smile or a favor, calling her their "elfin lady" until she fled to the city gates and out into the fields. After the third time of trying to evade them, she only went out after dark, after her father had retired, with the shadows to protect her. She learned to move silently and cautiously, and soon she was but a specter.

When she did not feel the desire to be among people, to listen to the way they spoke to one another and laughed and shouted and fought, she would exit the castle gates and walk in the empty fields. They were beautiful to her because she knew no others. The green, rolling hills of tapestries were flat and dull compared to the wide world outside her rooms. To the west of the castle stood a wall of naked trees, and she wasted no time in exploring them.

On one of these excursions she found a little-used path and followed it. As she pressed into the dark heart of the dead forest, however, color began to emerge. Green mosses crept up the trunks of trees. Broad leaves, dark and glossy, blotted out the sun above her. Fallen leaves burnished the path in orange. She bent to examine flowers she had no names for and stood on her toes to run her hands over the leaves and trees she could not identify. Ahead, she could see light where the path opened into a small glade.

Cygna took her shoes off to feel the grass under her feet, cool and cushioned. The blades tickled between her toes. She washed her hands and face in the stream. The water was so cold it hurt at first, but as she crossed it turned her feet pleasantly numb. At the center of the clearing was a stone with a hole at the top and spiral carvings all around. At the bottom was a dark stain that looked vaguely like a handprint. This was the place of the white hind and the Lady all in White that her father spoke of so often—the woman no one said was her mother, but she knew could be none other. Many times Cygna sought sanctuary in her mother's glade, as she called it, and always the path was waiting to take her there.

When Cygna did desire to be around people she would go into one of the town's many taverns to listen to the resident or traveling bards and the gossip of the locals. In this way she learned what her governess would not teach her; of her father's disinterest in rule and the blight that was spreading year by year. She disliked hearing them blame her father, and internally made excuses for him. Many of the minstrels' fairy tales she recognized from those her governess told her at night, though in less graphic detail. But as she attended more court banquets, new rumors erupted and spread and evolved.

"I heard tell there's some girl been seen hanging around the court lately. One arm. Moves funny. Won't talk to anyone."

"One of them spies from over the border, no doubt."

"What, a child?"

"Not unheard of."

"Isn't it obvious? It's the king's bastard get. Cygna, I think she's called. They said she's only got one arm. Seems she found her way out of the dungeons, plotting her revenge. We'll have a new queen this time next year, you mark my words."

"I heard she's one of them fae folk and she's got a wing to prove it, and fangs for drinking blood. That's why servants up at the castle keep disappearing."

"Superstitious tripe. She's only got one arm on account of being born the wrong side of the bedsheets. God's punishment."

"What about the fangs, then?"

The rumors about her were enough to drive Cygna back to the confinement of the castle walls, but even there she found no safety. Every room and every corridor was lined with tapestries, from new and bright to faded and frayed, depicting the conquest of kings over rivals, women, and gods. Several were dedicated to her own father's triumph over the savage Otherworldly King. Only there did she find creatures like herself, but like the fireside fairy tales, the stories woven into the tapestries showed only their perfidy and eventual dismemberment. Everywhere she turned, the threads depicted everyone who looked like her as a monster, and so she saw in herself something monstrous waiting to emerge.

When she burst into her quarters they were empty; her governess had slipped away to visit her family. Cygna threw open the chest at the foot of her bed and dug out the old dolls she had altered, now buried under the untouched, newer dolls her father still insisted on giving her, and smashed them to pieces. What future could she hope for when all the world around her was waiting for her to show her true nature? Yet she had no desire to torment, maim, or devour the people around her. Only two paths were open to her that she could see: one hidden away in these rooms with a wing she would rather chop off than keep twisted under her gowns, or one where she gave into what was waiting inside her and embraced the monster.

And yet there might be a third path. There could be another arm under all those feathers, Cygna reasoned in her desperation. An arm, a hand, fingers whose tips sprouted feathers instead of fingernails. She flexed her wing, folded it, curled it around her, but she could discern no difference between its capability and her other arm, save that she could grip nothing. She ran her fingers over those hated feathers—those blades of shimmering white that marked beauty and elegance in beasts but something monstrous in her. But for them, she could leave these rooms and walk among family and friends. But for them, she was human. But for them, she never need fear what lurked inside her. She grasped her outermost feather.

Perhaps underneath she really *was* human, and she need only make the choice. Her governess always insisted that she withstand the anguish of transformation to correct herself through prayer and self-discipline. Surely this was another way. A faster way. A sacrifice to please God, that He might wash her clean. She would do anything to make it so.

In a fit of desperation, she yanked hard on the feather and shouted at the sharp pain that shot up to her shoulder. She covered her mouth to stifle the sound, but no one came. If the guards heard, they could do nothing without a key. Cygna had a rare moment of being truly alone.

She stared at the crushed feather in her hand. The pain stung her eyes, yet there was some part of her that needed it. Not enjoyed it, but she felt she deserved it. That it somehow purified her of her fairy taint. She wove her fingers into her useless flight feathers, brushing them out, then yanked them away by the fistful.

She had to bury her face in her pillows, unable to stifle her shrieks and sobs. But as she tore away feathers in a fevered haste, the pain numbed to a dull throb. Spots of blood speckled her dress, her bed, and the growing pile of feathers around her. Her mouth filled with the taste of iron and salt as tears tracked clear steams down the blood on her face.

As the flesh beneath the feathers slowly emerged, Cygna tore more furiously, her sobs louder. Beneath was no arm but a skinny limb befitting a bird, bleeding and raw. The very air stung as it touched that horrid appendage. It was the truth she did not want to see; the hideousness beneath all those beautiful feathers. The same hideousness and lurked inside her somewhere, waiting to come out. All the stories said so.

Cygna tore the last feathers away in fury and anguish as a hasty key rattled in the outer chamber door. The guards must have heard and fetched her governess, for the woman exploded into the room amidst a cacophony of frantic calls. When she found her charge curled in a nest of bloody feathers, however, her concern turned to furious disgust.

"You took me from my family for this? We thought someone was murdering you, stupid girl! Stop your sniveling. On your knees for prayer!"

But Cygna refused and blows rained down on her neck, her shoulders, and her tender wing. When they did not stop her sobs, her father was sent for.

"This is why I ask you to stay in here," he said as she buried herself in shame under her quilts. "Only I love you for what you are. And because they don't understand you, they will try to hurt you. If they see you as you are, they will be afraid of you. They'll lash out at you. Best they think of you as simply malformed and armless. With such a disguise, perhaps one day you may rule in my place. Even then, if anyone outside this country discovers your secret they will see you as the evil queen of an evil nation. They will declare war on us to eliminate what they consider your pollution, and thousands of innocents will die as a result. You understand now why I ask of you as I do."

"I am one of them. What if I become cruel?"

"No. You are special, and I raised you right. You are strong and moral and clever. You got that from me. But you must trust me and keep out of sight when I say. No more sneaking around without your escort. No more talking to the queen or trying to reach your sister. They do not understand you. And you can't trust them to keep your secret. Even if they don't intend you harm, which we cannot know for certain, anything they might say will see harm come to you."

And because Cygna had never seen any reason to question what her father told her, she believed every word, and loved him for it.

CHAPTER THREE

THE SERPENT COMES TO CLAIM

The private war between king and queen had turned their attention from the ongoing problems of the kingdom. The pestilence that sickened livestock and withered crops sprawled to the borders, turning the country into a wasteland. No export to make them rich; no stores to see them through winter. The once proud kingdom now had to rely on the generosity of its allies to feed its population, though the royal banquet tables never felt the lack. Neighboring kingdoms worried the corruption would spread to their own territory, but the wasteland held firm at the borders and encroached no further.

Two decades from the first sign of the blight, a creature from the Otherworld appeared at the wasteland's edge: a giant serpent which wound its body around barrows and struck at passing travelers. The Lindworm, they called it, and its rage and hunger was matched only by that of the ruling monarchs. Every night it moved further into the kingdom, its trajectory fixed on the capital. Queen Gyda sent soldiers and knights against it, but steel glanced off its scales and its wounds healed with a speed that was nothing short of unnatural. It struck through armies and generals and left nothing but bent armor behind.

The Lindworm's imminent arrival at the castle and King Torvald's lack of action was not the only trouble on the queen's mind. Soon Cygna would be twenty and come of age to rule, and the king made no pretenses in his intention to abdicate his throne once his heir could take legal responsibility. What troubled Gyda was that he never declared which of his daughters that heir would be. In the eyes of his subjects, Aila was the only option. But the existence of a firstborn, never declared illegitimate, was the kingdom's worst-kept secret. Gyda did not know Cygna's mind; the girl might actually believe she had some claim, and she had the right to ask a boon upon her coming of age. What doting father could deny such a demand?

It was not entirely the ascent of such an unnatural creature to the throne that troubled the queen. It was true that a half-fairy ruler would be a sign to allies and enemies alike that the rot withering their country had eaten to the heart of the throne itself, and evil ruled. The already dissatisfied peasantry would see her as no different. Cygna was an untested and weak girl-child who could command no one's respect. Which conflict would swallow them first, civil war or crusade? But she feared far more personal repercussions to Cygna's ascent to power. There was no love between them, and both the queen and Aila could expose Cygna's secret. That made them a liability. With the young ruler newly crowned, the mother and her daughter would be superfluous. To Gyda's mind, it was a matter of her own survival to see that Aila was declared the true heir, and Cygna removed. If she could influence who came to power, she could influence her own fate.

When King Torvald's advisers predicted the Lindworm's arrival in the capital to be within the week, and the king turned from the problem yet again, Gyda took her opportunity.

"You can't leave every issue in the hands of your privy council," she said on the eve of Cygna's birthday. "You must act. The people need to see you act. What good are you if you won't fulfill the most basic function of a king?"

"They tell me steel does nothing against it. And you have burned all the witches who might have helped us. What action is there left for me to take? Leave me alone, woman. I will be taking my supper with Cygna."

"There are alternatives to steel, if you will only listen."

"I am exhausted of this responsibility. Tell my advisers."

"The Lindworm is a creature of the Otherworld you are so fond of."

"I cannot see how. You have seen to the destruction of every gateway left in our kingdom."

"Which means it must have found some other bridge. A connection between its world and ours."

"Then have it destroyed. Good night."

"The bridge is Cygna."

The king stopped in his retreat.

"She is a creature of two worlds that you were irresponsible enough to make, and to let live," Gyda pressed. "It is she who links our worlds together. Why else would it come now, when you are poised to place her on your throne? It has come to either champion her or take her back, and it will devour us as it does."

Torvald sank against the wall and pinched the bridge of his nose. "And I should take it on faith that her death would save us? I would trust you, and you would pour poison in my ear and cause me to kill my only joy."

Gyda laid a tender hand on her husband's arm. "I have never felt for her as you do; I cannot deny that. It is my resentment toward you that has always led me to tell you the truth, for I know how much it hurts you. For that I am sorry. Once your advisers understand the link between Cygna and the Lindworm, they will have you kill her. But I beg you now, stay your hand. Spare your daughter's life. There is nothing to be gained in destroying her. We can save her, and in turn she will save us."

"How? How do I save her from them?"

"The Lindworm is not the only monster that threatens us. Our allies threaten to withhold aid if we do not send soldiers for their wars. Our enemies send spies into our court to probe our weaknesses and discover the truth behind rumors of a demon daughter. And there is talk of a people's revolt against the crown. What good is a child monarch against all that—whichever daughter you choose to succeed you? I know you intend to name Cygna, but she has no claim as she is. She is a stranger. A broken little princesses no one will follow. But a queen of fearsome fae blood, one who championed your people against her own kind . . . that would command respect. And if you intend to proceed in your folly, sending her to confront the Lindworm is your only option."

"I will not risk her, not by sending her to face the Lindworm and not by exposing her nature. The result would be no different than if I wielded the headsman's axe myself."

"Her nature is our greatest weapon. If she succeeds, she will have proved herself worthy of your throne and win the hearts of the court. Allies and enemies will fear and respect us. What threat of civil war can there be with a creature such as her to keep insurgents in their place?"

"She doesn't have your ruthlessness."

"Of course she does. She is one of the Fair Folk. You may not see it, but she has preserved herself this long despite the many people within these walls who wish her ill."

"No. She will stay here with me. My advisers will think of something. It's their duty."

"If you do not send Cygna away to face it, it will come here and there will be nothing left of us. Not finger nor feather. Do not trap her here, as you have trapped me for more than twenty years, to become a withered husk of the woman she once was, or might have been. Let her discover the world for herself and seek the lands she came from. Whatever curse you have bought upon us, let her be the instrument by which you save us."

It was midnight when King Torvald relented, and Cygna was awake when he unlocked her door. She took the news of her imminent departure solemnly, and listened as he explained and made excuses for himself and laid blame on the queen over and over. She believed him when he told her she would return home unscathed. She believed him when he said he would ensure she would be sufficiently prepared.

Despite the initial flare of fear and anger, she did not protest. She had never questioned her father's wishes, and through the habit of years it did not occur to her to do so now.

Her birthday was spent not in celebration of her coming of age but in preparation. She was dressed in her usual fashion and presented to her father's privy council in formal declaration, both as his daughter and as their potential savior. Priests of every order arrived at the cathedral to anoint her. For Cygna, it only served to hasten the hour of her departure.

In late evening Cygna escaped to her rooms for solitude and her own preparations. As she laid out her least uncomfortable dress, she heard a key in the door. She hoped it would be her governess come to help dress her and not another priest with his blessing. She was only in her shift and had no armor between herself and prying eyes.

She waited for the door to open, but once the lock clicked there was only a hesitant knock. Cygna faltered; no one who visited ever bothered to knock.

"Come in?" That was something she'd heard her father say, surely.

The door opened enough to admit a slim figure. Even without her ball-room mask, Cygna recognized the princess by her royal dress and the way she moved; Cygna had spent a lot of time watching her sister from the Court's shadowed corners.

Whatever Aila was about to say was strangled out as her eyes drifted to Cygna's wing, naked and unbound. Six years had passed since she tore away at it and the feathers regrown, and it shimmered with the shifting light from the fire, a faint rainbow sheen moving over snow-white feathers. She immediately looked away again, red-cheeked, eyes darting to

Cygna's face, other arm, chemise, across the room to her writing desk with its pots of multi-colored inks, at the laid-out gown, everywhere but at that curious appendage. Her stare was vacant, her attention focused to the side and toward what she desperately wanted a good look at. She started to form words a few times, but clearly could not think of anything to say that was not about the wing.

"How did you get the key?" Cygna asked.

Aila glanced at her hands. "I had a copy made years ago but never had the courage to use it."

"Come to see if it's all true?"

"I'm sorry. I shouldn't have disturbed you." Aila turned to the door.

"I'd like you to stay."

Far from the calming effect Cygna had hoped her invitation would give, the girl turned pale and trembled.

"Are you . . . Do plan to eat me?"

"I beg your pardon?"

"When I was a girl, Mother told me you ate your wet nurse. And the stories say your kind—"

"No. I don't intend to eat you. I depart in a few hours and I do hate to leave a meal to waste. Besides, I'd rather not get blood on my feathers." There was no response but a suspicious look. "How am I supposed to have eaten a whole wet nurse? A babe with no strength and no teeth?"

Aila relaxed, arms dropping to her sides. "I always wondered that too. But Mother said it with such conviction that I questioned my own doubts."

"You believe everything she tells you?"

"And do you believe everything our father tells you?"

In the silence following, Cygna realized that it had never occurred to her to disbelieve him. He was her father. Kind and protective. "He said never trust anyone," Cygna said, "even you. That if I was caught, I'd be burned. Or disfigured because my deformity would upset people. Is that why you're here?" She stretched out her wing. "To take this away?"

Aila held out her empty hands. "I left my axe in my quarters." She indicated the dress. "Do you want help with that? A lady can't dress herself, wing or no." Aila flushed red again at her boldness in mentioning what she had previously been determined to ignore.

"My governess is coming to help."

"I waylaid her so I could come here. Sorry."

"Then I'd appreciate the help. Tie it loosely, please. I'm not sure I'll have help again when I need it."

Aila picked up the pieces of the gown and they worked together, Cygna showing her how to bind her wing in a soft swath before covering it with the shift.

"It looks painful," Aila said.

"It's not comfortable."

"If you come back, I'll sneak my dressmaker in to you. She'll make you something better suited."

"Thank you, but I would be afraid to wear anything else. And what do you mean, 'if I come back?' Father promised I would be perfectly safe."

Aila knelt with the skirt and let Cygna steady herself on her sister's shoulder as she stepped in.

"No one but Father expects you to survive," Aila said as she tied the last laces at the back of the bodice. "Mother only convinced him because she's sure you'll never come back. He wants you to be queen after him, and he thinks sending you off to your death will help people accept you. I hope he's right."

"You're not hoping for the throne?"

"I will be a queen," Aila said with startling resolve. "It's my birthright. But I have no intention of ruling this place which God has forsaken. I intend to marry well and become Queen some place far off from here. Don't ruin that for me." She turned Cygna around and inspected her work. Then she pinned her older sister with such a look that she resembled her mother. It made Cygna nervous. "You're the queen this country deserves. We need you to come back."

"I'm not sure I should take that as a compliment."

"It's meant as one. You seem nice enough, or good enough at seeming so. That will upset people's expectations. And with a half-fae queen, maybe we'll regain the respect we once had."

"Or our neighbors will declare us ungodly and wage a crusade against us. That's what Father says will happen if I don't play the part of a demure and, above all, *human* queen."

"Our father only cares about you, hunting, and making Mother miserable. He's not interested in doing what's best for you and this country—only pretending you're something else. He seems to think that's the way to keep you safe. And damn the rest of us." Aila spoke with a surety that hinted at a resentful acceptance of her lot. It made Cygna deeply ashamed, and she looked away.

"You sound like you want to hate me."

"I do want to. I have done. When I came up here I was sure I'd slap your pretty face. I hoped once you left, Father would have time for me. But… well." She signed, and her shoulders slumped. When she spoke again, her voice was softer. "It's easy to hate someone you've never met face-to-face, and boast about all the scores you'd like to settle. Even when they told me you didn't exist, I knew there was some ghost between me and my father. But now I've met you I realize I need to settle that score with him. Not you."

"I'm sorry if he's neglected you for me."

Aila opened her mouth to reply and abruptly snapped it shut again. "I should go before I'm caught here. I do hope you come back. It would be nice to get to know you. I think we could have been good at being sisters, had things been different."

"I'd like that."

"I'll leave the door unlocked so you can leave on your own terms. I've already seen to the guards." She opened the door but before she left, she looked back over her shoulder. "Happy birthday."

With Aila gone, the room was empty but not safe. It had been Cygna's sanctuary for twenty years but now it felt violated, as much the domain of her father as it was hers. She did not want to see him or suffer his abrupt and forceful entrance into her private world. She needed solitude. Her own secret key was still hidden in the music box on her bedside table, just where she had left it six years before. She might need it later. The old gray cloak that used to hide her was dusty and moth-eaten, but still serviceable. She looked like a servant under it, and that made her nigh invisible.

Thirty minutes of slinking through shadows later, and she was out through one of the castle's service entrances and into the town. Another half-hour past that and she was running toward the line of denuded trees that marked the edge of the King's Wood. She would come back for her final preparations, but for the moment she needed the solitude and comfort of her mother's glade.

CHAPTER FOUR

THE PATH HOME

The forest had always been a ruin in Cygna's memory. As her feet kicked up dust and she clambered over fallen logs, she wondered for the first time why nothing grew here anymore. What connection did that have to the king? The things her sister had said and scraps of overheard conversations from her clandestine tavern visits stewed in her head.

Cygna picked her way along a little-used path until the trees filled out lush and green and the canopy blocked out the moon. Through the wood's darkness and silence, there was a glimmer ahead where the glade awaited her. Once across the stream, she sat in the grass and breathed deep, pressing her forehead to the cool stone with its whorled carvings.

Finally, the nagging doubt that had been trying to get her attention burst full force into her mind: she was likely going to die. What had felt so abstract to her for all her father's rushed explanations was there in front of her. She was leaving. She was alone. She had no safety anymore. No one expected her to come back. The queen hoped she wouldn't.

Shortly before midnight, as the Swan Maiden knelt by the stone with the dew soaking into her skirts, she heard the familiar tread of her father crossing the glade.

"I have searched for this place for twenty years," he said as he knelt beside her. "Tonight the path appeared to me as if it has always been there."

"It always has been. I think it was protecting itself from your wife. And from you."

His face hardened, but she saw him overrule the brief anger. "I know I disappoint you; you think I am blind to the danger I am sending you into. But they have forced my hand. Else I would keep you here with me always. Safe."

"You say this Lindworm creature is expected to reach the castle within the week. There is no 'safe' anymore."

"It will all work out fine. It always does."

"You can't turn your back on the Lindworm and ignore it, just as you have clearly ignored everything else unpleasant."

"I have ruled this country well enough since long before you came along, young lady."

"By having someone else take care of its problems. As you're doing now."

"What has gotten into you? Why are you being so difficult? Everything I have ever done was for you. I am giving you up so you can have the freedom you have always asked for. Freedom to explore and to discover where your mother came from. Don't you understand how painful this is for me? How alone I will feel when you are gone?"

Cygna cast her face down, feeling it burn in shame and guilt. A small part of her mind shouted that he was turning her own anger against her, but she shut it away. She was not ready to face her doubts yet.

"I'm sorry. You have always put my happiness before yourself. Thank you for everything. And I will do my best, I promise."

"Ah, my beloved." King Torvald embraced his daughter, drying his tears on his sleeve. "I know you will."

"So my mother truly was from the Otherworld?" Cygna asked, wanting to change the subject and end the embrace.

"I met her in this very place. It was the happiest I'd been until you were delivered to me. I am sorry I didn't tell you anything of her before. I feared it would inspire you to leave me to seek out her kind. Your kind. But now, despite myself, I must send you back there." He handed her the satchel that hung on his shoulder. "In there you'll find enough food and water for three days if you use it sparingly. I expect you home in that time."

She opened it and sifted through the bread loaf, dried meat, and water skin.

"No weapon?" she asked.

"They tell me nothing can harm the Lindworm. You'll have to find some other way to defeat it, God help you. Seek out its source. Someone must have sent it, and you may have to kill them. I suspect their king. But who can resist such a lovely creature as you? He won't stand a chance against you. With him gone I can send an army into that wretched realm and lay it to waste to protect us from further harm."

He helped his daughter to her feet and brushed the grass off her skirts.

"I believe this stone is the last gateway into the Otherworld, but I hope you will have better luck trying to open it. The morning your mother disappeared I must have tried everything. I dug around it, shot arrows through the hole at the top there, I even attacked it with my sword. You can see a few faint chips here, along the side. I am not one of them, and I believe that to be the secret." He fixed his daughter with a keen eye. "But remember, you are not entirely one of them either, and you do not belong there. Do not give them your name, or they will have control over you and look into your soul and its desires to tempt you. Nothing around you is as it seems. And do not eat their food. It may look tempting, but it will turn to rot in your mouth and you will never come home. Above all, come home to me. I will have nothing left without you."

"I promise."

He embraced her again for what she feared might be the last time and took his leave. She looked into the satchel again. Three days of little food and water, and no weapon. Her doubts crept in again, but she numbed herself against them. She had no safety. But neither did anyone else.

Yet here she stood, at the hour of her departure, and she had already stumbled at the first task. She did not understand how she was supposed to cross from one world into another. Instinct had drawn her to this clearing and this stone, but how could a stone be a gateway?

Cygna stared a long time at the deeply cut whorls. The patterns spiraled like ripples in water, but came together around a central hole near the top. The same dark stain that so reminded her of a bloody handprint also darkened that void. She had no knife, but she'd made herself bleed plenty of times without one. With considerable effort Cygna managed to loosen her bodice, but her shift and the binding cloth were still too tight to get her hand under. She shrugged out of her under layers, too, and felt a sense of relief as she stood free and unswaddled in the cool night. She took a moment to stretch the muscles of her wing, stirring the air around her.

Cygna grasped a feather and, with a sharp pain that shot up to her shoulder, pulled hard. Blood splattered into the spiral pattern and onto the liberated feather — spots of bright red on white—and she placed it inside the hole.

Nothing happened for the space of a breath.

Then a breeze gusted through the glade and the feather floated free, spiraling to the ground. Where it settled onto the grass, there was a rumble and the Swan Maiden fell back as the earth opened into a pit of black. The grass and dirt sank from sight, loose soil and stones breaking free from the edges and falling into the dark without a sound, not even a faint thud of landing. Once Cygna was sure there would be no more landfall, she crept on her belly toward the cavern. A weathered ladder rose from the gloom.

So. It was not merely one of the Otherworld kingdoms she was destined for; it was the Underworld itself.

Cygna looked at her discarded clothes. It would be difficult to get the bodice back on alone, and she needed both limbs to climb down. She settled for putting on her rough woolen shift. It, at least, could accommodate her wing. The thought of going about with her wing exposed gave her greater pause than the prospect of being under-dressed. Surely in the Underworld there would be more like her—and yet she felt more exposed than when she'd stood naked.

Steeling herself, Cygna emptied the pockets of her discarded skirt into her satchel and slung it over her shoulder. With some difficulty, she lowered herself into the hole and climbed down. She gripped the side rail with her hand and wrapped her wing around to the back of the ladder to keep her balance.

As she began her descent, however, the top rung disintegrated and fell away. Cygna paused, wondering how stable the ladder might be. It did look very old and weathered. But the wood beneath her feet felt sturdy enough, and the rung she gripped held fast. She lowered herself again, gingerly testing the next step before putting her full weight on it. It held.

As soon as her hand let go of the second rung, it too crumbled to dust and fell into the darkness below. It was not the strength of her ladder that was being tested, but the strength of her will. She had not gone too far; it would be a struggle, but she could pull herself out again. To safety. Surely there was another gate between worlds.

Cygna had nearly convinced herself of her own lie, but could not bring herself to act on it. Suppose the gate closed behind her? She would return to the castle a failed woman, and the murderer of the kingdom as surely as any Lindworm. The shame itself would be the death of her, if not a mob and a burning pyre. It was the death she knew, and she would face the unknown death in hopes that she might find a means of escape.

Cygna descended, and the ladder crumbled above her as the starry sky slowly disappeared. She had no idea how cavernous or close the darkness was around her or how deep the pit below her. After what felt an hour of slow descent her arm shook as the ache of exhaustion set in, and she feared her grip would fail. What an ignominious end that would be. Her palm was slick with sweat and blood from splinters. She paused a moment to catch her breath, but the rung she clutched to crumbled and she fell away.

The fall was not far—she had only been a few feet from the ground. Dirt clung to the sweat on her face and shoulders. As she brushed it away, she noticed there was another source of light.

Standing nearby was a Knight All in Red and a Knight All in Black, each with a torch in hand. They flanked a set of great ebony doors carved with entwined serpents. One snake held a lock in its mouth. The knights bowed as she stood.

"Well met," she said with a curtsied response. She may be in only a shift, but it was no reason to forget her manners. "I am—" She stopped, remembering the advice of her father never to give her name lest it be used against her. "I am a traveler. May I please enter?"

The knights gave no response. It was not a refusal, so she pushed against the doors. They were firmly locked.

"Is there a key, good sirs?"

Again, they offered only silence. The Swan Maiden contemplated the doors for a moment. Behind the serpents were carvings not unlike those on the stone. Blood had unlocked the path above, had it not? She looked at her hand. A large splinter stuck in the tip of her ring finger. It came loose with a tug of her teeth and she spat it aside, resisting the urge to suck at the fresh well of blood to stop the sting. Instead, she placed her finger inside the lock in the snake's mouth. She heard the mechanism inside click and the doors swung open.

The cavern beyond struck her at first like her father's cathedral, long and high with pillars along each side. Except this was no godly hall. No human hand had shaped this place. The high ceiling was lost in what might have been smoke or mist, with pinpoints of distant light giving the haze a faint glow. Had she been above ground, she might even have mistaken them for veiled stars and clouds with a halo of moonlight. Glimmers of shining dust floating down toward her until her hair, shoulders, and limbs were covered in a fine layer, outlining her form in the darkness.

Set before each pillar was a brazier of embers or the last vestiges of flame. By their light, Cygna could just make out shapes carved into the cavern pillars, a rough-hewn attempt to emulate the grand columns of a kingly palace. Finely carved flora featured the tight spirals of fiddlehead ferns, the petals of clematis, and the leaves of ivy. The artisan's chisel had reached as high as it could before the carvings melded once more into the natural column of the cave.

As Cygna approached one pillar to admire the craftsmanship, she leaped back. A face had emerged from the stone leaves, staring at her with dead eyes. It too, was of stone, but of such lifelike texture and proportions that she at first mistook it for a living creature, and now was not entirely convinced that it had not started as one.

"We have expected your return."

Cygna whirled toward the voice. A woman stood beside her, her features obscured by the folds of cloth that wound loosely around her whole person. She was difficult to make out in the dark, the edges of her form seeming to blur and blend into the darkness.

The Woman Wreathed All in Shadow turned and bowed to the Knight All in Red and the Knight All in Black who stood inside the door. "Thank you for your vigil. Now she is home, your duty is done. You may go." The knights bowed in return and made for the far end of the cavern, where there was a glow Cygna could not quite make out.

"The ladder crumbled behind me," Cygna said, "and I have no way to get home."

Though she could not see a face, Cygna felt the warmth of a kindly smile. "Of course it did. You cannot return the way you came. After all, is the girl who started the descent the same as the woman whose feet touched ground here? There is a way back for you, but you must find it yourself." The warmth disappeared, leaving Cygna in a sudden chill as a distant scraping noise cut through the silence. The Woman Wreathed All in Shadow clutched Cygna's arm. "We must go, and quickly. This is not an hour to tarry. Come with me."

She moved swiftly down a side corridor, despite a slight limp, and the Swan Maiden struggled to keep pace.

"Is something wrong?" Cygna asked.

"It is not safe until sun-up. Here, go in this room and bolt the door. I will come for you in the morning."

"What is—" The door snapped shut in her face.

She put her ear against it, hearing the uneven steps of her guide retreat. Once they faded there was the scraping again, as of something heavy being dragged across the stone floor. No further footsteps; only huffs and snorts from an inhuman mouth. It drew nearer and for a heart-clenching moment Cygna thought it might stop outside her door, but it carried on. She released her breath and turned her attention to the door itself.

The wood was ancient, but the multitude of locks and bolts looked new. They were intended to keep something out rather than keep her in. There was no key, but Cygna took the key to her own bedroom door out of her satchel. It fit the locks perfectly. Safely barricaded against the strangeness outside, she sat with her back pressed to the wood and hugged her knees.

The chamber she'd been thrust into looked strangely like her own. At the center was a large canopy bed with heavy brocade curtains. The bedside table was laden with a display of fruits beside a music box. To one side was a writing desk with pots of multi-colored inks, jewel-bright, and a low candle burning.

The familiarity made the tightness in her chest ease slightly, but small details felt wrong. Her own door back home had no bolt; its purpose was to keep her in, not keep her father out. Instead of a fresh spring breeze, it smelled of damp earth here. The colors were too rich and the fruit too glossy and inviting. The room felt as though it was trying too hard to be homey and welcoming. She suspected that she, huddled against the door in her dust-stained shift, was the only real thing and if she fell asleep, she would wake in a bed of rotten straw and find the fruit withered and maggot-eaten. Hungry as she was, and tempting as it looked, she made do with the bread and water from her satchel.

Feeling better without hunger gnawing her stomach, she gave in to the temptation of the bed. It was warm and a bit too soft, and she sorely regretted that she had ever left the confines of her castle. She mistrusted the courtiers and their masks, and she did not miss the insults of her stepmother, but at least they were familiar. She knew what to expect. Here she could trust nothing, not even the reality of the bed beneath her or the prowling of the hunter outside.

PREDATORS AND PREY

Come morning, Cygna had slept little but she was started from her dozing by a sharp knock at the door. It took her a moment to remember that, while there was a resemblance, this was not her own bedroom. A faint golden morning light hung around the walls and the furniture but there were no windows and no discernable source, only a painted sun that she did not remember being on the wall the night before. In place of the fruits that had laden the table the night before there was a plate of breads and hard cheeses with a pitcher of cold, clean water.

The rapping at the door came again and when Cygna unbolted it the Woman Wreathed All in Shadow swept in.

"Good, you're a sensible girl. I feared you were the adventuring type and might go out in the night, despite my warning."

"What is out there?" Cygna asked.

"A curse gone horribly wrong."

"Is it the Lindworm?"

"Yes. I fear it sensed your arrival and came looking for you. But I have taken precautions. Here, I brought you breakfast."

"Thank you, I have my own food." She drew the provisions her father had given her from her satchel.

"That sad loaf of bread? It won't last you long. What a life you must have led to be so mistrustful."

"I was warned not to trust the Fair Folk."

"Your father's kind do like to make up stories about us. And about you."

"This place doesn't feel right. Like it is trying to force itself on me by wearing a mask, but that mask keeps slipping."

"It's trying to welcome you home. It wants to you feel as though you belong. Isn't that what you've always wanted?"

"And how would you know?" the Swan Maiden snapped.

"You are one of us walking among your father's people. That has never ended well for either side."

"I'm not the only unnatural thing up there. What do you know of the serpent that is ravaging my world?"

"Not *your* world, my dear. Not exactly. And *never* call yourself 'unnatural' unless you want a clip on the ear. There is nothing wrong with you. Stop using the language of others to describe yourself. Now, I am here to bring you out to meet your people—but that shift absolutely will not do. I don't know how they treated you back in that wretched place you've called home, but here you will have raiment befitting your station. I took the liberty of having this prepared for you."

The Woman Wreathed All in Shadow opened the wardrobe and produced a gown of deep blue velvet and samite with silver embroidery. When Cygna tried it on, she found that in place of the left sleeve was a veil of shimmering silk. The bodice tied at the side to accommodate her wing. As the Woman Wreathed All in Shadow cinched her in, she felt a prick in her eyes at this simple act of decency. She had many fine gowns at home that she was expected to appreciate. Here, the subtle flutter of sheer silk against her feathers enhanced and celebrated her form. For the first time she could look into the mirror and see a reflection she thought of as pleasing. Natural.

When the Swan Maiden was dressed, the Woman Wreathed All in Shadow stepped back to admire her work. "Beautiful. You look more like your true self now. And what shall we call you, my dear? Not your name. Your father knew nothing of you when you were born. What do you call yourself?"

Cygna hesitated. Despite her father's advice, she had not stopped to think of a new name for herself. Now, under pressure, nothing came to her.

"Forgive me," she said instead, "but it does not seem right to readily give my name to one who has not given me her own."

"I'm glad that your father's mistrustfulness has taught you some caution. That will serve you well, here and elsewhere. You may call me Runa if you like. And I have traveled in your world enough to hear you called 'Cygna.' That will have to do for now, though I can't say it's the name I would have given you. Like all things, it will change. I suppose it was appropriate that your father should name you for a hatchling swan. But you will not be a child forever, however much he may try to keep you so. Nor should you let anyone treat you as though you are. Come, we must introduce you."

Cygna did not have a chance to ask about Runa's curious comment on name choice before she was ushered back into the grand hall where she had first arrived. The change was extraordinary. What had been darkness and distant starlight was now bright and open. The cavern roof was lost in a fine bluish haze that might, from the corner of one's eye, be mistaken for sky. The braziers were roaring with open flames and between the carved pillars were tables covered in bright cloths and laden with food.

Filling the hall were tight clusters of people in fancy garb, like animals with human parts. Their faces, while not all human-like, did not appear to be masks, but Cygna did not trust that what she saw was their true form either. One man, whose legs were thin and backward-jointed like those of a beast, had a head wreathed in hair of fire with a flaming beard that dripped down a bare chest. A woman in a nearby group teased him by extinguishing the flames with a gust of crypt-scented breeze from the feathers in her hair. Cygna was unsure whether the raven feathers she wore were her own or an elaborate gown that covered every inch of her save her golden eyes, the matching paint of her lips, and her gold-tipped fingers.

"Is this how all the Fair Folk look?" Cygna asked. She watched a small figure, neither man nor woman and covered all in hair and leaves, who wove in and out of the clusters of people, speaking to them briefly and moving on. With every visitation the group would listen in rapt attention and be left either in laughter or tears. Cygna recognized the storyteller as one of the Woodbines from her father's tapestries.

"Hardly," said the Woman Wreathed All in Shadow. "A few of them are in their true form. The rest disguise themselves with glamours, but their affectations do not stand against scrutiny."

"They sound much like my father's courtiers."

"Those who fancy themselves above the rest are the same no matter what side of the veil they are from."

"And are you hiding your form as well?"

"I have many. Among them a white hind."

Cygna tried to peer into the woman's cowl, but it was as much use as trying to distinguish between shades of dark on a black night. The suspicions that had crept around the edges of her sleepless mind last night began to take shape.

"My father has told me stories about hunting a white hind."

"Stories have an important place and I could tell you many, but you have more important things to focus your efforts on. I cannot be selfish."

Runa brought Cygna forward to introduce her to a group of women whose gowns appeared to be living vines. "Ladies, I present to you Princess Cygna, a lost daughter from our lands."

In this manner Cygna was escorted through the hall and introduced in close company to a whirl of strange names and faces. The raven-feathered woman's touch sapped Cygna's warmth and made the world near her turn dark and close like the ancient tombs she'd read about. The flaming man's voice boomed like a blood-lust battle cry over ravaged fields.

When at last they reached the far end of the hall, the crowds opened into a bright expanse. The circle on the floor was richly tiled in a mosaic scene of two men, one robed in blue and the other in green, engaged in what might have been battle or embrace. A serpent with its own tail in its mouth ringed the pair. The crowd of Lords and Ladies, all so tightly pressed together, stepped not a foot in the circle. At the opposite side was an apse carved into the cavern wall, painted with a bright sun at its crest.

The apse housed an ornately decorated throne of gold with a young man seated upon it. His green samite doublet was vivid against his dark skin. The coronet upon his brow, like so many twisted branches of gold, rose in nine cruel spikes. A face far too young for such a heavy ornament was masked behind a neatly trimmed beard, and his curly black hair was swept back and tied at his neck. He sat perfectly still, eyes closed. Cygna tried not to stare openly but could discern no movement—not even the stir of breath or the flutter of an eyelid. Gazing on him, intense sadness and loss pressed around her heart as if to bury her in the earth.

"Is he dead?" she finally asked.

"Not quite," was Runa's reply. "Though it would be better for all if he were. Our king is under a curse. Should any try to rouse him, the Lindworm will hunt them and tear them to pieces."

"Why are all these people here? Surely they prefer the safety of their own homes."

"They are here to take advantage of his royal hospitality. They enjoy the king's food, his wine, and his musicians while carefully avoiding him. Come sundown, they will neglect their duties to flee like cowards and none will help him in his struggle. With no victims to devour here, the serpent goes above."

"Why my kingdom?"

"In part to punish the queen for burning our sacred groves. But the Lindworm is a creature of unchecked greed and wrath, and like attracts like. Cruelty comes in many colors, my dear. It can be possessiveness, just as it can be neglect. I hope you will remember that when you return to your father's castle."

"And does the king wake to battle the Lindworm every night?"

"I think you will find him helpless against it."

"If the king can do nothing, why has it not killed him?"

"It will eventually. And then there will be no safety for anyone, above or below, night or day. Come, let us return to your peers. I fear we have already drawn too much attention to ourselves."

Cygna did as bidden, if reluctantly, and allowed herself to be swept again into the swirling dance of courtiers as they ate and laughed. The Woodbine came to tell her the story of a girl married off to a murderous man. As she listened, Cygna forgot she was in an underworld kingdom. She was now mistress of a grand house, discoverer of the fate of her husband's previous eight wives. She mastered herself against her fears, however, and fashioned for him a garment so splendid that he would be the talk of the Court. Into each of the nine pieces she sewed a scrap of dress found on his victims, as well as her own. Into each scrap she sewed one of his many vices. His vanity could not resist, and each night she preserved her life longer as he waited for her to sew by weak lamplight, her needle-pricked fingers dark with both her blood and that of his former wives. On the final night she presented him with all nine pieces and bade him try them on. As he donned the final piece, his form twisted and shrank, becoming a rat which she picked up by its tail and threw in a vat of lye.

Relief and joy swept through her and she receded again into the King's Hall, surrounded by light and color with the face of the Woodbine smiling up at her. As she gave her thanks, the storyteller pressed something into her hand and slipped away to the next group.

The Swan Maiden felt her spirits much improved from the night before, yet her eye constantly strayed to the Sorrowful King on his golden throne and her heart felt heavy for him. The painted sun in its apse was low to the horizon now, a moon rising opposite, the light in the hall tinged orange. The crowed thinned, and the Woman Wreathed All in Shadow sought her out.

"We must retire soon, else risk becoming prey."

Cygna agreed, but cast one last look at the king entombed in his apse. She broke away and walked swiftly toward him. As her foot crossed into the mosaic, the Knight All in Red and the Knight All in Black appeared to bar her way. The crowd behind her fell silent, all eyes upon her.

"Let me pass," she commanded, leveling an unflinching glare. She had never been so forceful with anyone, and she had to admit it felt good. She so rarely stood against anyone.

The Knights' helms moved a fraction toward Runa; then they withdrew their weapons and bowed away.

Cygna approached the king. With every step, sorrow weighed her down until she could scarcely lift a foot. Once she reached the dais she was close enough to study him, and she took a moment to admire the sharp angle of his features, the subtle changes of tone in his dark skin, the long lashes that fringed his closed eyes, and the neat trim of the beard that framed beautifully curved lips. He could hardly be much older than her, but the Fair Folk, she knew, were not to be judged at first glance. She curtsied.

"Thank you for your hospitality, My King," she said, and turned away.

The ashen faces that greeted her on the other side of the mosaic also turned aside, none deigning to meet her eye but the Woman Wreathed All in Shadow. Cygna wondered what expression that hidden face wore. She said nothing, however, merely put her arm around Cygna and hurried her toward her quarters.

"I am locking you in tonight," Runa said once they arrived. She took Cygna's key from the desk and pocketed it. "I admire your compassion, but you do not understand the needless danger you have put yourself in."

"Do as you must," Cygna said. "I am used to being locked out of the way."

"This is for your own good."

"Yes, I've heard that too."

Runa hesitated, then cupped Cygna's cheek. "I cannot protect you; I know. I hope to find you here in one piece come morning. I am so sorry." The door closed and Cygna heard the heavy click of the lock, then footsteps moving away.

Cygna sat on her bed and fortified herself with salted meat and water from her pack, waiting. She watched the little painted sun on her wall. Like the sun and moon in the king's apse, during the course of the day it had made its arch over her bed. Now she watched it sink beneath the painted horizon, and the light in her room slowly changed. She waited a bit longer. Finally it was full dark and she had to light the candles to see by. It was her time.

She took from her pocket the object the Woodbine had given her. It was a key, fashioned from silver with a single wing at the top. The storyteller's skills of perception must have seen how the events of the evening would unfold; it was a gift Cygna knew most storytellers possessed.

She had not yet reached the king's hall when she heard again the heavy scraping sound from the night before. Up ahead she could see the pillars of the vast cavern. In the shadows, a movement—a glimmer. What she had thought a wall shifted, reflected the firelight. Scales like sapphires slithered out of sight. Cygna froze, unable to make herself go further. Her breath came in sharp gasps and sweat beaded on cold skin.

Ahead, something rumbled, then shrieked. Cygna flinched, feeling its volume and its pitch vibrate in her bones, and sprinted back to her room. Behind her the Lindworm shrieked again, crashing into the corridor wall in chase. She did not look back; she did not need to. Her chamber door was slightly ajar, and she rammed her shoulder against it, slamming it closed and throwing the bolts behind her.

Silence pressed in around her and weighed on her chest, squeezing her noisy heart and lungs. Had it gone past? Cygna was about to put her ear to the door when she heard a scratching at the wood.

"Sssssignaaaa . . ."

She heard her name spoken as quietly as a breath. A hiss. She covered her mouth to suppress a sob. The scratching continued, louder. More insistent. She could feel it through the wood. She heard her name again.

"Go away," she hissed back, trying to keep the tremor from her voice.

The Lindworm let out another loud shriek and threw itself against her door. The dust of ages burst from the wood in a yellow cloud that sank slowly to the ground. The second blow brought with it a few splinters. The bolt shot back. Cygna threw herself forward to force it into place, but a third blow sent such a shock into her shoulder that her arm went numb. There was no stopping it getting in. She had failed at the first trial. This would be the end of her, the end of her father and her sister. The end of the Sorrowful King, for whom she hadn't even spared a thought when she had fled in her terror.

The serpent on the other side rammed against the door again, the hinges and remaining locks threatening to give. No, she would not let this be the end. Too many depended upon her. There was nothing with which to defend herself but the voice of command.

"Hold!" she shouted, and it echoed at her from the stone walls. No further blows assailed her door, so she continued. "I will bargain with you, Lindworm, if you will listen."

A beat of silence, then: "Yessss . . ."

"You must be exhausted of your nightly hunt. Everywhere you turn there is blade and fire to meet you. But—" She swallowed, knowing that if she did not stop herself from saying the next words, they would change her. "But I can bring you the woman you seek to punish. The Queen Above."

There was no taking the offer back. She felt her blood turn a little colder.

"I have little interest in her," the Lindworm said in its quiet voice. "It is you I hunt. You, whom so many blame for their misery. You, through whom I will punish the woman who made me."

Cygna's tongue felt thick and dry, but she forced out her next words; she had forced herself into a corner and could see no other choice. It was her reward for offering the life of another.

"Then I will meet you willingly. Tomorrow night, alone and unarmed. I will end your strife, but in return you must promise to kill nothing tonight, Above or Below. Do we have a bargain?"

A pause. "Come out now, and I will leave your family in peace."

"No. I need the day to put my affairs in order. But should you devour anyone in that time, our deal is broken."

"Very well."

Cygna held her breath as she listened to its unmistakable bulk dragging through the corridor with a rhythmic scraping. The Lindworm was retreating to the King's Hall. Once again, she threw the bolt that had seemed so large and unnecessary the night before. She would not go out again tonight; if she met the creature face-to-face it might devour her then and there, bargain be damned. So she stripped off her gown and crawled into the bed that tonight felt warm and soft and homey. No fears or worries stood a chance against it, and soon she was dead asleep.

CHAPTER SIX

LAYER FOR LAYER

When Cygna woke again the next morning, she felt groggy with too heavy a slumber. The day felt late, and indeed the painted sun was well past its zenith. Her stomach rumbled, left empty for hours. Perhaps Runa had knocked and Cygna had slept through it. Perhaps she was presumed dead.

She slipped back into her dress with ease and even managed to cinch it herself. She could not tie it one-handed, but found special hooks that locked the laces tight, as if the dress had been made especially for a one-handed girl. Cygna was not sure if she was discomfited or warmed by the idea of a dress made for her before she had even known she would be coming.

The King's Hall, fit to burst with the gathered Court, fell silent as she entered. She bore down their open stares with a lift of her chin. Presumed dead it was, judging by their shocked expressions; best to make the most of it.

Courtiers parted as she made her way to the apse at the end, stopping at the mosaic's edge. If the king had moved in the night, there was no proof of it. There he sat, rigid still, eyes closed, nine spires of his crown glinting in the light. Not a hair nor fold of his garb was out of place. She curtsied to him and turned back to the staring nobles, who hurriedly went back to their food and drink.

Runa drew up to her.

"Well done," she said. "This lot won't underestimate you again so soon. That will benefit you, should you stay among us."

"If I survive the night."

"You must, or the king's heart will break. You have given him hope; do not take it away. With a broken heart he cannot hold back the Lindworm any longer."

"And how can you know?"

"Because you have given *me* hope. It was my curse that was the cause of all this. I could not control it, and I thought myself punished with our king. And so I wreathed myself in shadow. But my true punishment was to see you entangled in all this—that it would be you the curse chose, and it would not let you go. It has gone far beyond anything I intended."

"I made a bargain with the Lindworm last night. I promised myself in exchange for an end to its hunt."

"Tell me exactly every word that was said."

Cygna repeated what she could remember.

Runa sighed. "Words must be chosen carefully here, and are never to be taken lightly. You should have commanded it not to hunt, rather than not to kill. It breached your father's castle last night."

"I knew it couldn't be trusted!"

"No terms were broken. No lives lost, but it took your sister's left arm instead. I wondered why when I heard. Now I see it was a message to you of the consequences of a broken pact."

Cygna bit back sorrow and guilt and nausea. Try as she might to push the scene away, she couldn't stop it playing out as walls crumbled and her family ran to safety. Aila stalked in debris-strewn halls. Cygna flinched at screams of fear turned to shrieks of pain, saw Aila's tear-streaked face, her rosy-gold hair turned red. Her sobs quieted, weaker, as she waited alone in the rubble. Waiting to be found. Afraid she never would be. And all of it Cygna's fault, because she had not spoken more carefully.

"Then it honored the agreement, though it certainly found a way between my words. And I must do the same." Cygna shook the horrors of her imagination away and clung instead to her anger. She looked up at the Sorrowful King. Even from here she felt the weight of anguish upon him, felt it mirror her own. She could no longer pretend that it was only her promise to her father that compelled her. The

Underworld King was tied to the serpent, and it might be with him she found answers.

"Tell me of the king."

"He has not been a king long; tonight will mark a year and day. As a prince he was the younger son. He was cruel and spiteful and jealous of his brother the king. He used to play such tricks. His final trick was the deadliest and whether the prince intended it or not, his brother's life was the consequence. Following the funeral, the prince took his place as the new king.

"The night of his coronation feast I stood before him and spoke the words that cursed him, and the Lindworm came to punish him by laying waste to his kingdom. Words spoken have power here, but they can be twisted against their speaker, as you have already discovered. He who craved power and recognition now suffers, powerless—for, struggle as he might, he cannot stop it."

"Do you believe he regrets his actions?"

"He has held the Lindworm at bay for this long. But I suppose you will find out tonight what sort of man he has become." Runa reached out and pressed Cygna's hand. "When you face the Lindworm tonight, your only chance of survival is to wear a dress of nine layers. Promise me."

Perplexed, Cygna nodded. "Where shall I get the other seven? I have only this and my shift."

"The ladies of the Court are unguarded. I'm sure you're clever enough to find the rest you need. I will make sure no one comes to find you." The Woman Wreathed All in Shadow glided away.

Cygna looked around at the collected Lords and Ladies. None would look at her directly, though several regarded her from the corner of an eye or through downcast lashes. Curious to know how she had survived the night, yet afraid to be targeted through association, no doubt. In her pocket she could feel the weight of the Storyteller's key. Well. If these people would not help her, she would help herself.

The key, she discovered, changed shape for every door she brought it to. Seven ladies' boudoirs she entered, and seven shifts she filched from their wardrobes. They were easier to tear open to accommodate her wing than the ball gowns that hung beside them.

With the deed done and the last door re-locked, however, she felt a searing pain in her hand that shot up her arm and spread through her body, causing her to shout and crumple. Where her ring finger had been—the same finger whose blood had unlocked the serpent door two nights before—was a smooth, healed stump. The key was no more a sculpted lump of silver but a denuded finger-bone, clean and white.

She dropped it in horror, clutching her hand. The pain was already gone; only the memory of it ached. The noise from the King's Hall had receded with her scream, but no one investigated and for that she was grateful. Face streaming with tears, she gathered up the fallen under-dresses and hurried to her room.

The food on the table was now roast game with a pitcher of black-red wine. The smell of meat sickened her but Cygna poured the wine into a goblet, her hand shaking so badly she splashed it over the rim and onto the table. She knew she shouldn't drink it, but she desperately needed to steel herself, and as far as she was concerned, she was already damned. She gulped it down, then a second cup.

If she stayed in this place for long, she feared she would lose herself piece by piece—assuming she survived the night, and she still wasn't clear how that was to happen. She allowed herself a moment to think that she could leave. That she could find a passage out and flee home. Then she shut those thoughts away. Two kingdoms rested on the outcome of this night, but she couldn't think like that either. Instead she thought of her father. Her mother. The Sorrowful King. Poor, blameless Aila who suffered for Cygna's cowardice. If she had not fled at the first sight of the Lindworm last night, this could be over. Either she or the Lindworm would be dead, her sister unmaimed. She could be home, or on her way there, or at rest.

The last thought gave Cygna pause. Did she want to go home? It didn't matter now; there was little chance she'd see the morning. But if she did, what then? She saw no future for herself Above. There was only what her father wanted: duty. Responsibility over a country in turmoil. Bearing all that burden with no help from her father.

Ah, but here . . . She did not have to hide here. She could make her own future here. Come to terms with her mother. Come to know the king.

And if she did stay, her father's heart would break—and she did not think she could live with the guilt.

Once she heard the courtiers abandon their gluttony and hurry past her room, Cygna shuffled out of her fine dress and scrubbed herself clean. Once her skin was red and her feathers gleamed, she put on the rough woolen shift she had arrived in, still discolored with dirt. Over it she donned the seven stolen shifts, and finally her blue and silver gown. She felt stiff and heavy with so many layers. Fortunately, the ladies of the court had no need for warm undergarments and wore thin slips of delicate silks and linens.

The Lord and Ladies had evacuated the King's Hall long before the prospect of darkness; the only people Cygna encountered were the servants who rushed to remove the banquet tables and detritus of so many nobles feasting. They were so desperate to perform their duties before the Hunting Hour that they either did not notice her or did not care, as long as she wasn't in the way.

The painted sun in the king's apse was low and red, and the light of the hall had a bloody tinge to it. Cygna approached the throne to make her obeisance to the king. At an impulse, she reached out her hand toward his but did not touch him. She could feel his warmth, and that was enough. She bent her lips to his ear.

"I have come to free you."

When she straightened again, she saw that his cheeks were wet with tears and she sensed that, had he the power of speech, he would tell her to run. Instead she stood over him and took a moment to further study the face that had shaped her reveries—that face which she always kept within glancing distance wherever she was in the hall. She committed every detail to memory. The contour of his brow, the lines at the corner of his eyes, the shape and color of his lips. She was far closer to him now, close enough to touch, to feel the warmth of his skin. Her heartbeat made her ribs ache. She wanted to reach out and trace her fingers over his handsome face, to brush away the stream of tears. But she would not. He was too vulnerable like this. Too easily violated.

Her father wanted him dead. It had been a mere suggestion at the time, but she had heard the motivation behind it. He had sent her to kill the Sorrowful King, to make way for an invasion, and did not care how it changed her. She had already offered up her stepmother with barely a second thought, and that had been a ruthlessness she hadn't known she was capable of. Could she kill an innocent man?

Was he innocent? He was beautiful, certainly, but that was not the same thing. The queen was proof enough of that. Cygna supposed he was as innocent in all this as the rest of them, which meant hardly at all. But what a loss it would be if his death proved to be the Lindworm's undoing. If he had to die before she could know him. Before she could hear his voice, see his smile, or feel the warmth of his hand. If she had to kill him, now would be the best time, before she got too attached. But if it were to be done at all, she would be sure to remember his face.

Her father whispered in one ear, the Lindworm in the other. But she would not damn him for either of them; not until she knew his role in all this.

Cygna waited until the painted sun in its apse slipped past the horizon. The bloody light shifted to the long silver shadows of moonlight. The Lindworm's hour had come; time for the Underworld King to open his eyes and meet hers. To speak to her, take her hand and answer all her questions. Then she could decide if she obeyed her father or herself.

Nothing happened. Perhaps he would not wake until the Lindworm arrived. And when it did, it would not be wise to have her back turned. Disappointed, she descended the dais and stood firmly between man and beast. She'd hope to speak to him before she faced the serpent. She doubted there would be a chance afterwards.

Cygna waited, but there was still nothing. No scrape of scales, no breath, not even a shift in the air. She risked a glance over her shoulder.

The Sorrowful King's throne was empty. The hall held no evidence of him, nor of his nemesis. Climbing the steps again, she investigated the vestiges of the apse's prisoner: a pile of neatly folded clothes.

Cygna froze as she heard a soft sound close behind her. Perhaps it was the king. Something teased the hair at the nape of her neck and sent a warm shiver through her. So he had come to her after all.

She raised her hand to take his, but with a snarl came a gust of hot air against her skin. The warm feeling in her belly turned to ice that radiated out to her limbs, making them heavy and numb. A great toothed maw emerged from over her shoulder.

The Lindworm had her in its coils in an instant, dragging her bodily from the dais. She scratched and scrabbled at the tiles of the mosaic. More coils looped around her, and she was lifted to its face. Nine golden horns crowned his sapphire head.

The Lindworm King scrutinized her as he squeezed the breath out of her. He opened his jaws, and she held her arm over her head. His teeth sank into the nine layers of her dresses, barely scratching her skin. The serpent roared as he came away with nothing but a few threads, and she stole the opportunity to reach upward. If she could grab one of his horns, she might pull free of the coils.

Her hand found purchase, and she pulled hard. The gold spike broke away and the Lindworm King roared again. As he made for another bite she lashed out, the broken horn rending a tear in the scales of his face. He dropped her and she rolled away.

"You promised yourself to me," he hissed, "and you seek to trick me with enchanted cloth. I have already tasted your sister. Strip your layers, or I will make a meal of her instead."

Cygna got to her feet, halfway between defiant and demure. But it was Aila's life or hers, and that meant her choice was already made.

She reached for the laces under her wing, but the Woodbine's story colored her mind. "Only if you promise to shed a skin for every dress I remove."

"And why would I do that? It was not part of our bargain."

"Those are my terms. I will not fight you; that is my promise in return."

"Very well. I can see no harm in it." He stared at her expectantly, blood from his broken horn dripping off his snout and splashing at her feet. Finally he shook his head angrily, widening the tear in his scales and wriggling free of his skin.

His new scales shone glossy and iridescent, a greenish tint to their once deep blue hue. Cygna thought of the Woodbine's story, and of the promise she had made to the Woman Wreathed All in Shadow. Layers of cloth for layers of skin; one for each vice that had made him, and which spoiled her own country, to change a man. To change them both. She understood her instructions.

Cygna shed her nine layers and made him match them. She realized now that her gown had been Possessiveness, followed by the first shift, which was Selfishness. Next she challenged him to Arrogance. He grew weaker with each skin shed. Soon Greed and Recklessness joined the vestments on the floor, followed by Cowardice, Cruelty, and Conceit.

Soon Cygna stood in naught but the rough woolen shift she had arrived in, and the Lindworm curled and panted before her. His scales were translucent now, and she could see muscles and distorted limbs beneath—his true form trying to emerge. He dragged his towering bulk toward her and bowed his bleeding head with its broken crown. She broke away the remaining eight spires and used them to cut away his final skin, because he had no strength left. He waited, expectant, and she slid Self-Pity from her shoulders and let it pool around her feet.

The king gave a low, mournful howl and collapsed, shattering the mosaic. The great serpent's body disintegrated, leaving the Sorrowful King curled naked in a pile of emerald scales. He did not stir, nor draw breath.

Cygna edged close to him and put her hand to his breast, hoping to feel a heartbeat. She had achieved the first task set upon her by her father, to stop the Lindworm King. But had she also fulfilled his ulterior wish, and in so doing failed herself? Had she freed the Sorrowful King by killing him? Cygna bowed her head as tears stung her eyes. She had fought to preserve him, and instead she had lost him. She would never know what sort of man he had become while he struggled against himself night after night. Who had won in the end, the man or the Lindworm?

Cygna felt around for her warmest shift, the rough woolen thing she had worn closest to her skin, and named it Compassion as she laid it over his body. She followed it with the silk of Kindness and the linen of Sacrifice. Then she kissed his eyes and collected her ruined gown, retreating to her room.

The soft padding of her feet and the dragging of her dress were the only sounds until her foot struck a twisted lump of metal. The wreck of the king's crown flickered with torchlight. It would make an excellent trophy if she ever made it home; proof of her triumph over the King of the Underworld. She would have it reforged and made into a crown of her own when she took her rightful place as queen. Cygna held it in her hands, felt its weight, and pictured herself in the seat of power. She had never deluded herself with hope, but now rule was within her reach.

And once she had the picture clear in her mind, she realized that she wanted none of it. It was not a responsibility she cared for. And so she tossed the twisted crown in a nearby brazier and went back to her room to fall into a heavy sleep. Her father expected her back on the morrow. Come morning, she would search for a path home.

CHAPTER SEVEN

UNBROKEN

When morning came, however, Cygna woke to a pounding on her door. It did not cease as she dressed herself in what remained of her gown. It was not Runa, as she had expected, but the Knight All in Red and the Knight All in Black.

They escorted her wordlessly to the King's Hall, where the Lords and Ladies greeted her with serious faces. She had killed their king and must receive justice. The only way out of this world, she realized, would be to leave her body behind.

The silent crowd parted for her as they brought her toward the apse. On the broken mosaic was a pile of chopped wood under a roughly built platform. A stake stood out from the middle. Cygna stopped when she saw it. She had accepted death many times in the last few days, but there had always been a hope she might escape it. Now it stared her in the face.

"Lady Cygna, I am glad to see you have not fled our realms."

She looked up to the throne, where the king sat in splendid raiment of green robes trimmed in gold. They hung open over his chest, exposing the rough woolen tunic with smudges of dirt that he wore next to his skin. In place of his golden coronet, he was now crowned with a wide expanse of antlers formed by a pair of blooming saplings. The tip of each branch burned with a candle-like flame.

The Knight All in Red and the Knight All in Black took their place at his right hand. The Woodbine Storyteller already stood at his left.

The Underworld King's eyes were open and fixed on Cygna. "We feared you would leave us after your ordeal." He raised his gaze to the Lords and Ladies. "Who among you looked beyond your own greed and cowardice to raise a finger against our curse? We have all let others die in our place and are equally to blame, save this woman here, a lost daughter of our lands. While you feasted, she bled for you all." He looked back to her. "It is easy to be cruel, and I know it better than any here. Kindness requires sacrifice. My Lady, what would you ask of us? Any heart's desire. You have but to ask."

"This is too much, Your Majesty," the Swan Maiden said. "Please, let me be on my way."

"You do not wish to take your place among us?"

"I have a duty to return. I would see my father, as promised."

The king's head lowered, his voice quiet. "Then you must leave us, and do as your heart bids."

Cygna bowed to the handsome king, heavy regret weighing her down, wondering if she would be able to find her way back here. She reluctantly made to leave, but the Woman Wreathed All in Shadow appeared from the recess of the apse. As she stepped into the light, the darkness that had clung to her dissolved in whorls of smoke and she was once again the Lady All in White. Her steps were small and tentative as the king turned on her.

"You have been the cause of our suffering," he said. "And for that you will burn. Take her to the pyre."

"If I may, Your Majesty," Cygna said, "do not make your first act of your new reign be one of cruelty. The purpose of my mother's curse was to teach you to be otherwise."

"And in so doing she nearly brought both our kingdoms to ruin. She must not go unpunished."

"Just so, Your Majesty. As such, you cannot claim sole punishment. As the only representative of the Kingdom Above, I demand half the sentencing."

"And what do you suggest? I will not have her under my rule."

"And I will not hand her over to my father. Let her return to that place between our worlds—that place where she made me. There I may visit her. But never again will she step foot to either side without explicit invitation and escort. That shall be her punishment and reward for the lives lost through her curse."

The Lady All in White stood immobile as her daughter meted out judgment and as the king examined her.

"I can see the justice of it," he said after an uncomfortable silence, "for through her actions we have met you, and that is worthy of reward enough to save her life. Does anyone in my court object?"

A tense silence followed, and no one raised their eyes. Cygna wasn't sure exactly which of the three of them they were most afraid of.

"Very well," he continued after only a breath. "Your own knights will escort you and see to your protection."

Runa bowed low. "Thank you, Your Majesty. And thank you, Cygna. I am sorry I had to give you away. I hope you can understand that. For all you have done here, and for sparing my life, I would give you a parting gift. But first some advice. Your father's warnings were not without merit, but not all were specific to the fae. Discard your name. The power of names is not in the having but in the giving. Those who gave it to you will seek to control you by it. Name yourself to ensure that no one else has power over you."

"Thank you, Mother."

"Now your gift. We respect your need to return to your father's kingdom. Promises were made, and you intend to keep them. It is your home, and it will always draw you. But you have eaten our food and drunk our wine, and as such will always pine for this place. And when you give in you will search for us again. Without a key you will find yourself trapped in the mists between our worlds, wandering ever after." She produced a small box which contained the finger-bone Cygna had discarded. "This will open any door, fling wide any gate."

"I can return here?" Cygna asked, hope stirring in her breast. The king, too, sat up again.

"You may come and go as you please. But the crossing is never easy, and it will take its toll on you and leave you restless. The love you leave behind, Above or Below, will pain you. Each time you leave one for the other, you sever yourself. You may choose another gift: forgetting. Take back this finger, heal your hand, and choose one world. You will forget the love that binds you to the other, and the painful ordeal that goes with it. But once your finger is on your hand, it can never again be used as a key. You will never again have need of it."

Cygna glanced at the clean stump on her hand. To feel no pain was a mighty gift. No guilt for leaving her father. No regret for leaving the Underworld and all its marvels, where she felt more acceptance and belonging than among mortals. No draw to the beautiful king and all he offered. She looked up at him, but he looked away with a face that betrayed his breaking heart.

"I will remain severed and restless. The pain my memories bring has helped shaped who I am. I have always been a woman born of two worlds, and I would not change that."

"You will come back to me?" the king asked.

"It will please me to do so."

He smiled briefly, then composed himself and addressed the Court once more. "Leave us. Everyone."

He waited in silence until the hall was empty. When even the servants and the knights were gone, he stood and descended the dais to stand before Cygna.

"Thank you," he said. "As you can see, my Court is bereft of selflessness. It is long since I have experienced true generosity." He raised her hand to his lips. "I will be glad to see you when you return."

"What is your name?" she asked.

"I don't know anymore. I am searching for a new one. Perhaps you will help me."

"Would that not give me power over you?"

"I wouldn't mind." The king released her hand and took instead her wing, smoothing the feathers and brushing away dried blood. "You have transformed me back as I wished to be. That bond grants me the power to transform you in return. Do you wish to be rid of your wing?"

She shook her head without hesitation. "No, I shall keep it. I may have desired to be rid of when I was young and in despair but, for all the stories people tell, there is nothing wrong with me. Nor do I have to fear becoming those stories. They were not written by people like us."

"Then I can give you another wing and you shall fly."

"I should like that very much. But no. Thank you. I would like to stay as I am. Not severed, but unbroken."

"So mote it be. Instead of a Broken Princess you shall be the Unbroken Queen... if you will consent to rule at my side."

"I do not want rule."

"Not even with someone to help share the burden?" She did not answer. "If you will not consider rule, will you at least consider me?"

"Not yet. I don't know you. But I think I would like to."

CHAPTER EIGHT

A FLAME IN THE DARK

Three nights Cygna stayed with the Underworld King. On the fourth morning he took her along the path that would lead her to the edge of her father's kingdom. All other gates within its borders were destroyed, and she could not go back the way she had come.

"Have you thought of a name?" he asked her as they prepared to part ways.

"I like 'Sigune'. And have you chosen one for yourself?"

"Not yet. I won't go back to the throne when you leave me. So much of me was devoured by the Lindworm. Dismembered. I would like to travel a while, learn a few things about who I have become. My kingdom did not collapse while I was cursed; it can survive without me a little longer. When I have re-membered myself, then I will choose a name, and hope that when I see you again you will like the man I discovered along the way."

He reached up and, with a grimace, broke away one of his sapling antlers. "You will need this. Both to undo the damage of years and as proof. You are an uncomfortable truth, and they will do all they can to hide you from view. Make them see you."

She took the bough, cradling its slight weight with her wing. Despite the flames, she only felt a comforting warmth. The same warmth she felt near him.

"It wasn't rule I wanted," he said. "Only recognition. But my selfishness cost lives, and a king's selfishness will manifest in his kingdom, be it above or below. Remember that when you present this to your father." He kissed her cheek. "I will miss you, Sigune."

She frowned. "I may stay with 'Cygna' for a little longer."

"Of course. A name is a difficult habit to give up. But you will come into it."

She embraced him, breathing in his earthy scent. "I will think of you."

Only the broken bough of the king's crown lit the end of the path, and Cygna, who could not yet think of herself by her new name, was glad to have it. As she took step after cautious step, she could feel the space around her constricting, and she only just saw the low stone ceiling in time to duck. Ancient limestone slabs narrowed in around her and she had to hunch to continue, holding the branch awkwardly ahead of her as she scraped her shoulders against the walls. The passage ended abruptly, a pile of stone blocking the end.

Behind her there was nothing more than a chamber like a beehive of stacked limestone. Three small alcoves held carved stone bowls of charred remains and in the central chamber, laid out in peaceful repose, the bones of some forgotten ruler were wrapped in a fur cloak with carved antler pins and ringed with pieces of quartz.

If this was the way she'd come, there was no way she could have avoided tripping over them, yet they were undisturbed. The air was still and stale and damp, the chill of the earth sapping the warmth from her limbs. There was no way into this tomb, and no way out. From no discernable source she felt the air stir again, as of the tomb exhaling, carrying with it the comforting scent of the Underworld.

Cygna turned back to the narrow passage and pushed against the piled stones that blocked the only egress. She expected nothing, but they fell away easily, and with them the avalanche roar of hundreds more as the face of the cairn slid away. Sunlight stabbed into her eyes, which ached even after she closed them. She gave herself some time to adjust before she crawled out of the tomb and into the open.

Though Cygna had never been permitted out of the castle to travel and see her father's country for herself, she knew the maps well. A wide river carved its southern border. As she emerged back into the sweet-smelling air of sky and daylight, she knew that must be where she had arrived. Where she stood, the hills were verdant. It was warmer here than in her home city, and though it was still early in the year, spring was already showing in the buds that swelled on the trees. Wood anemones bloomed on the verges of the road that led to a bridge across the river. The water sparkled blue against the closest shore but was clouded with mud as it neared the opposite shore.

The land on the other side of the river was in stark contrast to the life she felt thrumming in the very earth here. There, it was as though the soil had been sown with salt. If there was grass, it was yellow and dry. No birds sang in the barren tree branches. Fences had fallen into disrepair around unused fields. Looming over that opposite shore and its murky waters was a gray town, its docks overcrowded with fishermen whose lines were still and whose nets were mostly empty.

Two soldiers stood guard on the bridge nearby. They regarded her warily as she approached, having watched her emerge from the cairn.

"Will you let me pass?" she asked when she reached them.

They glanced at each other, at her wing, and at the flaming bough she cradled. They looked up at the cairn.

"We're only meant to keep people from coming the other way," the younger one muttered to his partner.

The more seasoned of the two kept his eyes on her, speaking from the corner of his mouth. "If it wants to make life even harder on them, it'll have its work cut out for it."

Cygna considered pointing out that she could hear them perfectly well, but kept her slight smile fixed in place. They shifted uneasily with the attention.

In unspoken agreement, they stepped aside. "Go on, Fairy, do your worst."

"You can't do much worse than their king already has," the younger man added. "But . . . the red-haired girl in that town there. What do you want to leave her alone?"

Cygna turned her gaze on him, and he flinched.

"Do you bring her and her family gifts of food?"

He looked down and muttered something that sounded like "Only her."

"And do you prevent the townsfolk crossing this bridge to forage?"

"We have to," the older soldier said. "Orders."

"I see. I will spare your sweetheart in exchange for the both of you providing an escort to any who want to cross and gather food. If you do not, you will both slowly wither from your toes to your navel, powerless to watch the onset of your own destruction, just as you watched these people experience the same." She brandished her branch at them, taking more than a little pleasure in how they hurried to get out of her way.

This had been a trade town, once; Cygna remembered that from her lessons. Once a thriving hub, now quiet. For years there had been nothing to export. Not long ago, any remaining imports had been cut off as the neighboring kingdom exerted pressure on her father. No one manned the gates of the town wall. There was no point; there was no one to come or go. She stared at them a while, then wandered off the road and into one of the abandoned fields.

No one had bothered sowing a crop in what looked like years. Not even weeds grew, and the soil was churned to mud by farmers' boots, and probably those of soldiers. Her father's knights had no doubt come through here in search of her mother, and the queen's knights in pursuit. And who knew what foreign forces had tested these borders?

In the center of the field, at the top of a small hill, was a stump. Cygna knelt to dig a hole beside the dead tree. She broke off one branch of her flaming bough and pressed it into the muddy depression, building up soil around it to make it stand. As she admired her work, she realized how much the candle-tips of her lover's gift looked like blossoms. She wondered if it would grow, and made a mental note to come back next year and check on it. For now, it would serve to mark her journey's beginning. She wasn't quite sure why, but it felt important.

A few people had gathered at the gate to watch her, and they stood firm when she reached them. A man dressed in magistrate's garb blocked her way.

"Leave our village in peace, demon. We have enough trouble. Undo whatever you've done and go."

"I am the Princess Cygna."

"What, the king's fairy bastard?" He looked again at her wing, scrutinized the join of her shoulder where skin gave way to feathers. She was wearing another of the Underworld gowns in red and gold samite, which she had chosen to wear without a chemise so that her shoulders were bare. It made her smile to remember how naked she had felt in her shift before, wing exposed, as she now proudly bore this man's examination of her form.

"Dear God. It's real. And you're real. God save us." He said it more to himself than her, and she tried not to be offended. He met her eye again. "We'll give you a room for the night, Your Highness. Forgive us for the mistake; we did not know you. You find us in a sorry state, but you shall have every comfort we can offer." Though his tone was placating, he did not look any happier than when he had thought her a fairy demon. Now she was a fairy demon he had to bow to.

"Where is your baron?" she asked as he led her into the town proper.

"Called to the capital. The Lindworm's dead, or so they tell us. I heard of no battle, but no one's seen it neither, not after it breached the castle. So they're feasting. And we're here."

"Did the news say how it was defeated?"

"I hear the king gave his daughter to the damn thing and it went away. We assumed it was the Princess Aila, but we didn't think you were real. But no one's seen her in days, either."

Cygna's gut clenched. The rumors could be about either of them. Yet another unforeseen consequence of her failure to stand against the Lindworm on that first night.

They arrived in the square that had once housed a thriving market. All that remained were the scales at the center, empty and rusted.

"There's an inn there. The owner will make you comfortable. You'll be wanting to move on in the morning, I expect." It was not a question.

"Yes, I would like to get home."

He nodded and led her inside.

Come morning, the tone with which Cygna was greeted was much warmer. A great commotion was taking place outside, and she heard men running and livestock braying. The inn was deserted. Outside the town wall, a woman hitched a donkey to a plow.

"Everyone is scrambling to get seed in the ground, Your Highness," someone answered when she enquired what the commotion was about. More confused than before, Cygna wandered in the direction the flow of people was moving, past the dilapidated fences and into the fields.

In the center, the branch she had planted the night before was now the size of a small tree. Pale pink blooms weighed down its boughs, and fallen petals carpeted the freshly green hill. Scrawny oxen, draft horses, and every other creature that could be hitched to a plow were being prodded through the fields with villagers trailing behind to press seeds into the furloughs.

Spring had returned from the Underworld.

The magistrate spied her and ambled over. "Your Highness," he said between gasps of breath. "You are a gift to us. We can never repay you for it. Seeds are sprouting faster than we can plant them. At this rate we'll have a harvest in a couple of months. My children will have a proper meal for the first time in their lives. I don't know by what magic you did this, but I pray God it's the good kind and He doesn't mind."

"It is a gift. Don't squander it. And I will make sure my father doesn't, either."

"You can't walk all that way. You'll have a horse."

"You can't spare it."

"There's a young one hasn't been trained to the plow yet. You'll have her. And my nephew and niece as an escort."

"Only if they don't object."

"They need to see the world. I suspect you're just what they need." He bowed. "Princess Cygna."

"I have taken a new name. Sigune."

The magistrate nodded. "It's a good name for a queen."

She returned his respects and went back out into the road: the road that would take her back to her father's side. This was only the edge of the wasteland. Ahead of her, to the horizon and far past it, was nothing but dry brown earth and barren trees. She knew it would be worse the closer she got to the castle. On the road ahead would be more towns, more villages, more farms to revivify. She examined the bright bough in her hand and counted the branches, the twigs, the flames. How many people could she save? Was the one bough enough to bring life back to the whole country? And could it stand against the power of the rot that spread from the throne?

She accepted now her father's greed and neglect, the possessiveness over first his queen and then her, that had made him ignore all else. It was a poison in him, and the poison had seeped into the land itself.

Behind her, the river glittered in the sun as fishermen hauled heavy nets from the water. Against the riot of green that now covered the hills, the town seemed less gray. Her escort, the siblings who so wanted to explore beyond their town, were laughing and running through the new grass toward her, a young chestnut mare in tow. She wondered if her own sister even lived.

Sigune looked ahead again, at the waiting road. Her feet touched hard-packed earth, but soon green shoots erupted in her footsteps. Behind her was an ever-widening path of new growth. Making her way to the capital would take a fortnight if she stopped at every hovel and every village on the way. Between the journey and confronting her father, bringing life back to the land was the easier of the two tasks before her.

She would cut a swath through the wasteland and stab at its heart. She loved her father, but he was the one who had poisoned the throne. And no king who turned himself from his people could be permitted to rule.

I may have abused my career as an academic in the acknowledgments section, but the truth is this story never would have been written in the way it was without my education as a mythologist. Constructing a new fairy tale isn't just about inventing a princess and giving her a few talking animal companions. Rather, it's a complicated layering of cultural and personal complexes. Some writers are able to tap into that inherently; had I tried to write this same story ten years ago I would have failed to give it the depth it needs.

The problem with the fairy tales we have recorded from a century or more ago is that they were meant to be an oral tradition and had differences between them depending on the region and era of their telling. 'The Six Swans' did not begin and end with the Brothers

Grimm,[1] nor is there any one true version of King Lindorm. Just as there is no one true version of Persephone or the Brisingamen or any other world myth. These stories were created and retold and altered to suit the needs of their individual and cultural audiences. Even their collection and publication were a socio-political act; the Grimm Brothers were looking for pre-Christian traditions to build a unified German identity, whereas Hans Christian Andersen collected those same traditions with the intent of bending them to reflect Christian morals. The result is a surviving body of cherry-picked versions concretized in ink, and thus we are now poorer for having lost the fairy tale oral tradition. Who knows how the stories might have evolved up to the twenty-first century?

Modern publishing has been a great boon to the fairy tale tradition. With the ease of publishing ebooks, something like oral tradition has come alive again, and as a result the fairy tales of old are coming alive, too. Red Riding Hood is able to rescue herself again.[2] Princesses don't just wait around to be married, but go off on adventures of their own. They even reject the prince if they want to. Fairy tales are,

---

[1] Also recorded by Hans Christian Andersen as 'The Wild Swans.'

[2] As she did in the pre-Grimm version as recorded by French folklorist Paul Delarue.

once more, reflecting the needs and the culture of the times.

As they did for so many fantasy writers, fairy tales played a large part in my formative years. I distinctly remember an illustrated book my mother used to read to me of 'The Wild Swans.' On the very last page, when the princess is saved from the pyre and she in turn saves her brothers from their curse, one brother is left with a swan wing in place of his arm. In the illustration all the men are gathered around their sister in celebration except for one, who stands aside looking at his wing with a mournful expression.

That image of the one-winged curse has stuck with me for decades and likes to resurface every now and then. At my first year of Pacifica's annual masquerade ball, I went as the Falcon Cloak from Norse mythology—rather, as someone in the process of turning into a falcon after putting on the cloak. At the end of the night there I was, all other costume pieces cast aside, with a homemade wing strapped to my left arm. Again. And suddenly I had a character I wanted very much to write about. Not a Swan Maiden of the transformation tradition, but some poor girl trapped between two worlds. And it struck me that such a beautiful creature would be deemed monstrous.

After all, of all the monsters of myth and folklore, how many behave in a way that is genuinely wicked, rather than acting on hunting instinct or in self-defense? We are told they are wicked and that is what makes them monsters. Medusa lives on an island because her gaze turns people to stone. 'Heroes' travel there to confront her and suffer the consequences when she acts in self-defense. The myths tell us that Medusa is a monster and we cheer when Perseus kills her. But what specifically about her is monstrous? What, when it comes down to it, is a monster? Something abnormal? There is certainly a long-standing history of people demonizing even the slightest differences. Is a monster, then, something that invokes fear? Something that acts aggressively? But there is a difference between aggressive behavior which is part of defense or natural hunting patterns, which is a very animal thing, and aggression for the sheer joy and cruelty of it, which is a very human thing indeed.

One of my favorite monsters who truly is monstrous is King Lindorm[3] of Scandinavian folklore. The story has slight differences between countries, but at the heart of the narrative, King Lindorm is a human trapped in a serpent body. He is angry and self-righteous and greedy and he delights in inflicting that anger and cruelty on those around him. It takes a clever girl who refuses to be devoured on her wedding night to strip him of those traits and break him down to his barest self before he can be redeemed as a

---

[3] Also called a 'Lindworm.' Both are derived from the old Norse word for 'snake' and refer to a giant serpent.

worthy monarch and husband. It is a gruesome and brutal process, much like the psychological trauma we go through when we do the same.

Fairy tales are far more complicated than we give them credit for.

I wove many motifs into *The Serpent and the Swan*, each one from the traditional stories, such as toxic monarchs, symbolic animals, and investiture/divestiture. Each one is a key part of the redemption arc,[4] a near-universal trait in these stories. Most fairy tales have a character who needs redeeming, be it the princess who saves herself or the king who needs a good smacking.

One might wonder why there is so much royalty in fairy tales. It wasn't just because they were the considered standard characters of what made universal entertainment, like the cis-straight-white-Christian-male of today. In fairy tales, Kings and Queens are symbolic of the culture, and the state of that culture is reflected in the state of the kingdom. In 'King Lindorm,' the Queen ignores the advice of the very crone whose advice she sought and takes more than she is meant to have. This greed indicates an imbalance in the kingdom itself. The poison starts with the Queen, as it so often does (the effect of sexual politics in the evolution of fairy tales), and it continues

---

[4] In the personal and cultural sense of the word, rather than religious.

in her firstborn son. He must redeem not only himself but, through him, the kingdom.

It is important that the Lindorm is, despite the story's title, a Prince. He is on the cusp of his inheritance, and his successful marriage marks this threshold. This is a period of rebirth, just as princes in fairy tales represent kings in a state of birth.

The Lindorm is redeemed through divestiture and, depending on the country of origin, beaten or washed with lye or any other number of horrible tortures. He is stripped of his essence and broken down to his most basic components. Clothes in fairy tales can represent the persona, the version of ourselves that we put forward to interact with the world around us. They are the version of ourselves we show the world, much like a mask. Multiple layers represent multiple attitudes, and the one closest to the skin represents the most intimate/personal attitude. Removing a layer of clothing can represent removing a part of ourselves that has become false or corrupted, removing our illusions or delusions, or removing our old self and exposing our true selves we usually keep hidden, making ourselves vulnerable like the snake who has recently shed its skin.

In Western Christianized symbolism, we might well assume that the serpent in the story represents evil. However, like most fairy tales, the 'King Lindorm' probably has pre-Christian roots, which means we must move past conditioned prejudices and look at alternative interpretations. Like the stag with its antlers, the snake sheds its skin on a regular basis, and this symbolizes renewal. And yet the snake's venomous quality also makes it the stag's diametric opposite. Unlike antlers, which regrow, the snake sloughs of what is dead to reveal the new layer of delicate, tender skin that is already there. Both make themselves vulnerable in the process, but (in the terms of a psychological interpretation) the stag drops and renews personas whereas the serpent sheds it perceptions—its way of interacting with the world around it in a way that was no longer useful and perhaps even toxic. It is a form of transformative death: that mythologem known as the Underworld journey, or *nekyia*.

With this research in mind, it felt only natural to me that the image I kept picturing of the cursed king on his golden throne was a king of the Underworld, and that his curse was serpentine in nature. King Lindorm, already noted as a personal favorite of mine, was a natural fit. And the Swan Maiden who redeems him is on her own redemption quest. Therefore the problems of the Underworld are the same problems that have caused her own kingdom to wither into a wasteland: greed, possessiveness, hubris, self-righteousness, etc. She is animalistic in her qualities, meaning she is a step away from the culture that she was born to. She is closer to nature, which could be interpreted as being closer to purity. Though I, as the author, would never insult Cygna by suggesting she is 'pure.' But she does stand outside society and has a different interpretation looking in at it. With the logical motifs in place, the actual plot easily fell in around it.

For all these high-minded cultural and psychological interpretations of fairy tales and the motifs I have borrowed, the only interpretation that matters is that of the reader. What resonates with one may not resonate with another. We have our own complexes, our own moral interpretations, our own ideas of what these motifs mean. I can excitedly repeat all the research that went into the construction of a new fairy tale but what matters is that it meant something to you. And I hope it did.

This book exists because my grandmother Carol Pym, who is traditionally a career-oriented woman, sat me down and gave me a stern talking-to that I was wasting myself on a traditional career. At the time I was an academic, and not very happy about it. I've been writing in one form of fiction or another since I was four and she wanted to see me wholly dedicated myself to what I care most about. So this section of thanks really needs to start with her. The book is dedicated to her, after all, and it is my privilege to publish it on her 94th birthday.

Of course a book is only as strong as its editor, and Emma O'Connell (www.emmasedit.com) made this one much stronger than when I gave it to her. Thank you also to James C. Bassett, proofreader extraordinaire.

Being married to a writer isn't the romance the movies make it out to be. Despite this, my husband Tom Gorman manages to survive, and with aplomb. He makes a remarkable sounding-board when I'm brainstorming and has quality input that always inspires something. And he's always there with pictures of red pandas when the writing goes wrong. Thank you also to my parents: Tom Jensen, Deborah Pym Harowitz, and Jack Harowitz. I lucked out in the cosmic dice roll.

My writing has seen a great deal of support over more than a couple decades. Michele Schutte is my longest-standing writing partner and has suffered through a lot of dreck. Sorry about that. I once promised I would dedicate my first book to her—sorry about that too. Following her, my old writing critique group in my native Seattle helped many a manuscript (and by extension me) improve, as well: Shana McKibbin, Justin Nafziger, Julia Nolan, and Julie Etheridge.

Finally, thank you to my writing mentors at Western Michigan University, Dr. Steve Feffer and Dr. Arnold Johnston, and to the professors at Pacifica Graduate Institute whose classes provided the base knowledge for creating a fairy tale, Dr. Evans Lansing Smith and Dr. Dennis Patrick Slattery. I may have made a terrible academic, but your lectures made me a better writer.

Ashland Pym made her debut in the theatre where she won a few minor awards and delighted in tormenting characters, actors, and audiences alike. After taking a break to get her MA/PhD in Myth and Psychology, she returned to fiction with a blend of dark, contemporary, and historical fantasy.

Pym has been a shepherd, a stage manager, and a volunteer for collecting otter droppings (which is how she met her husband). She dabbles with myth in academia, couches it into fiction, and lives it in her tiny woodland cottage in Connemara.

www.ingramcontent.com/pod-product-compliance
Lightning Source LLC
Chambersburg PA
CBHW030752110726
47900CB00008B/2574